PRAISE

"Graverobbers Gates and Holt have unearthed a set of tales that arouse and revolt, with more than a shovelful of humor. If you let these stories gnaw on your brain, you'll come away not only entertained, but with meaningful reflections on the most challenging aspects of human experience—love and death. I prescribe *Rigor Amortis* to you, STAT." —John Cmar, MD, podcast voice actor for *ESCAPE POD*, 2007-2010 Parsec Awards Judge.

"This new anthology gives fresh meaning to the term 'a nice romantic dinner.' Whether you're a connoisseur of the erotic or the grotesque—or enjoy a hearty helping of both—*Rigor Amortis* delivers a full menu of startling, horrifying, and even heartbreaking stories to whet your appetite." —T. M. Camp, author of *Assam and Darjeeling*, and *Matters of Mortology*.

"You'll barf, you'll cry...
... You'll also have your preconceptions challenged.
There's real sweetness in amongst the putrescence, and some humor, and some fine storytelling. Worth a read, certainly, but possibly not just before dinner—because some things really shouldn't go 'squelch' like *that*." —David Devereux, author of *Hunter's Moon* and *Eagle Rising*.

RIGOR AMORTIS

EDITED BY
JAYM GATES
AND ERIKA HOLT

EDGE SCIENCE FICTION AND FANTASY PUBLISHING
AN IMPRINT OF HADES PUBLICATIONS, INC.
CALGARY

Edge Science Fiction and Fantasy Publishing
An Imprint of Hades Publications Inc.
P.O. Box 1714, Calgary, Alberta, T2P 2L7, Canada

Cover Illustration and Design: Robert "Nix" Nixon
Interior Illustrations: Galen Dara and Miranda Jean
Layout: Brian Hades
ISBN: 978-894063-63-0

EDGE Science Fiction and Fantasy Publishing and Hades Publications, Inc.
acknowledges the ongoing support of the Alberta Foundation for the Arts
for our publishing programme.

Alberta Foundation for the Arts

Library and Archives Canada Cataloguing in Publication

Rigor mortis / edited by Jaym Gates and Erika Holt.

ISBN 978-1-894063-63-0

1. Horror tales, American. 2. Erotic stories, American.
3. Short stories, American. I. Gates, Jaym II. Holt, Erika

PS648.H6R53 2011   813'.08738083538   C2011-901626-5

Printed in Canada
(o-20110413)

www.edgewebsite.com

JAN   3 2012

CONTENTS

ROMANCE

REVENGE

RISK

RAUNCH

BIOGRAPHIES

INTRODUCTION

JAYM GATES

Zombie erotica; not your supermarket SPAM. It all started with a joke on twitter. Such is the beauty of the modern age.

I still don't know how it really came about. But I mentioned a possible for-the-love anthology of zombie erotica, mused about the possibility of shopping it to publishers, and a few brainstorms later, the project suddenly had a full head of steam.

I was fortunate to find Erika. Not everyone is up for undead sex, especially not the sheer quantity of a slush pile. Erika threw herself whole-heartedly into the endeavor, and we haven't slowed down since.

I really couldn't have done this without her, nor without Galen Dara and Miranda Jean, our talented interior artists.

Editing this anthology has been a short, strange, furious ride. Starting with justifiable concerns that "zombie erotica" could only be "zombie rape," we went out of our way to solicit and select stories with unusual plots, elegant characters, and lush prose.

We saw expected trends, unexpected trends (second person point-of-view!), and overall, a trend of phenomenal writing. With both first-time and established authors, we had a hard time choosing, mulling over the table of contents until the last possible moment.

This is not a collection for the faint-of-heart! There are stories in here which will thrill, amuse, disgust, and challenge. From tender love stories, to undead sex-trafficking, to voodoo, the stories run the gamut of style and emotion. Horror, fantasy, urban fantasy, science-fiction, straight-up zombies, gay, straight, and orgy, there aren't many unturned stones. Such is the beauty of flash fiction: bite-sized.

Just think of *Rigor Amortis* as a nicely-wrapped box of zombie appetizers. Brain, spine and spleen, there's something in here for everyone.

INTRODUCTION

ERIKA HOLT

A few years back, while working as a civil litigation lawyer in the lofty confines of a large firm affectionately known amongst articling students as, "the Death Star," little could I have imagined I'd end up editing an anthology about zombies. Or sex. Or graphic, zombie, sex.

You see, I'm not the type to jump up, arm waving, to volunteer for others' hair-brained schemes, especially ones that are provocative. So, naturally, when Jaym Gates, a person I knew only through brief contact on twitter, offered me the opportunity to co-edit an anthology of zombie erotica, I said, "Absolutely!"

It was one of the best decisions I've ever made.

Who wouldn't want to work with the tiny but fiery bundle of creative energy that is Jaym? Or an amazing group of talented authors and wonderful artists? I thoroughly enjoyed the editing process, whether it be debating how a vulva is best described; whether "cock," or..."*member*...," would work better than "dick;" or staring at stunning pictures of naked, rotting, and sometimes dismembered body parts.

Does that mean there's something strange about me? Jury's still out.

Luckily my husband has been very supportive, promising to foist books on unsuspecting work colleagues, though he's non-committal about reading it himself. But, how am I going to tell my mom? My in-laws? My...dad? Oh, God, my dad. And, my grandparents can *never* know.

But, regardless of what anyone thinks, I gained what feels like an encyclopaedia's worth of knowledge, (and not just about biology, though there were lessons there—when was the last time you used "mons" in a sentence?), and am extremely proud of what we've achieved.

Have fun with *Rigor Amortis*; I did.

RIGOR AMORTIS

AND YET IN DEATH

LANCE SCHONBERG

In life my love turned every head she passed,
She paled the moon and shamed the starry sky.
But when she failed, those gathered 'round me asked,
How God allowed such light to wane and die.
And yet in death her beauty still remains,
Oblivious to all my sobs and cries.
My careless tears upon her sheets leave stains,
Until some damnéd curse bids her to rise.
To seek out living flesh to slake her thirst,
She stalks the streets for any breathing thing,
Without a care she's somehow driven, cursed
To feast upon fresh hearts and brains. She sings
The joy and taste of still warm flesh. A kiss
Now spiced with blood and death, I can't resist.

Lance Schonberg lives in eastern Ontario, Canada with his wife, children, feline overlords, and a growing menagerie of small pets. Previous careers include bookseller, cubicle dweller, number cruncher, and craps dealer. His work has appeared or is forthcoming in a number of print and online publications.

ROMANCE

DELIVERY DAY

JACOB RUBY

Angela sat at the dining room table with a pink toolbox, a sealed cooler, and a disheveled stack of papers before her. She drummed the fingers of her left hand, her good hand, on the loose sheets of the printed manual, worn from reading many times. She'd intended to read it again while waiting, but found she couldn't concentrate. Instead she watched the street, waiting for the truck.

And thought of Jane.

Jane had been everything to her, for too many years to count. But obviously Jane had been counting, and eventually wanted someone younger, more pliable. They had stayed in touch—though the term friends was a stretch. Jane pretended to care, but her occasional presence brought mostly pain. Angela believed it had caused her stroke.

Her heart leapt into her throat as a large white truck pulled past, slowed, and began backing into the driveway.

The wooden crate looked heavy, but the delivery guy handled it just fine, sliding it to the platform on the back of the truck, then hand-carting it with ease to the front door. She met him there, holding the door open with her lame right shoulder.

"Hi, uh," he stopped, looked at her, then his clipboard, and then to the numbers beside the door. "Is the man of the house home, or, um, a son perhaps?" He kept his face down, searching for something more on the delivery sheet.

"No, that's mine," she answered. She watched his face flush a light crimson, and wondered if her nervousness showed. "Could you carry it in for me?"

He backed the dolly over the stoop, and wheeled it into the dining room.

"This is my third delivery today. More than a dozen this week," he said, still blushing but also smiling. "You're the first woman I've delivered to, though. Just doesn't seem like, um, well, something you'd get into, you know?"

She knew, and agreed. Before she'd left, Jane had told her about a new craze; like a sex doll, but so much more. Not quite alive, not really dead. Jane had suggested it could help around the house, but Angela knew Jane, always the dominant, had more in mind. Angela had refused. That didn't interest her in the least.

"Would you be able to help loosen the lid?" she asked.

"Certainly, ma'am." He seemed a tad too enthused.

She handed him a thick, flat blade screwdriver and a small hammer from the toolbox. He made short work of loosening the long staples, then began to pry-off the lid.

"No!" she said, stopping him. "I'm sorry, but that's enough. I can get it from here."

His eyes showed disappointment, but he smiled when she handed him a twenty. She walked to the door, thanked him again. Locking the door behind her, she stood for several moments, looking at the box.

A perfume smell drifted out, cloying in its fake sweetness. She understood its purpose, and it brought her back around to the task at hand.

She lifted the lid, let it fall to the back. The inside was lined with thick foam and filled with pink packing peanuts. A few strands of blonde hair peaked out. Lighter than Jane's. She scooped out the material, one handful at a time, slowly revealing a young woman, seated and hunched over.

Naked.

That hadn't occurred to her. She ran to the front windows to draw the shades down, into the living room to cover the back windows, and finally pulled the vertical blinds across the glass doors in the kitchen.

The girl had sat up and turned her head towards Angela, but otherwise was in the same position as before. Angela stopped; stepped back instead of finishing her stride. The girl's eyes, once a bright, steel blue, were now clouded over. They didn't track Angela's movements but floated around. Her nostrils flared, and her mouth moved slightly beneath layered strips of pink duct tape.

Angela grabbed the cooler. The bonding process required quick action, and she was prepared. She removed the tape, barely noticing the faint warning symbols across its surface. She pulled a raw cow brain from the cooler. The girl moved with surprising speed, grabbing the mass and gorging. Angela offered a second, trying not to watch but unable to close her ears to the violence.

That could be me.

No. The manual had said: *Feed them often at first, a diet rich in brains, and they will obey your every whim.* Angela understood the implication, but her whims were different. Now that Jane was gone, she *did* need help around the house.

After finishing, the girl became still once again. Angela cleaned her with a damp cloth, carefully wiping her mouth and chin.

"We should get you some clothes," Angela said, standing up. The girl followed her lead and rose. Angela tried not to stare, but the girl was flawless. Early to mid twenties, athletically thin and fit, long, naturally blonde hair; exactly as she had ordered her. Much like a young Jane.

Better than a young Jane.

Angela couldn't help but notice certain, other assets, ones she'd not specified: the full, high breasts, and the tuft of pubic hair, also blonde, waxed into a heart shape.

"We need a name for you."

She hadn't been planning to name her, but now it felt right. She took the girl's hand in her good one, found the skin cool to the touch. Angela pulled slightly and the girl responded, stepping out of the box with far more grace than she'd expected.

"I think I'll call you Lily."

The girl's hand squeezed hers and it felt...nice. Angela smiled at where her mind was going.

And blushed.

Jacob Ruby lives in Kansas City with his wife, who is also a writer. He received his BFA in painting, is a 3D illustrator and animator by trade, and spends the rest of his creative energies working on sci-fi, fantasy, and horror stories.

ALWAYS AND FOREVER

JAY FAULKNER

She's at the door. Still.

I don't have to look down from our bedroom window, though the full moon will illuminate everything in pristine detail and let me see her clearly. I don't need to go downstairs and peer through the back door, to our perfect little garden where the autumn leaves carpet the lawn with red and gold.

I don't need to look; I know she's there.

She's been there for the last three days. The last three nights.

Nights are the worst. It is then I miss her most. In the two years since we got married, we'd never slept apart. The same ritual, from our first night together to our last, always the same: undress each other and climb between cold sheets which would warm beneath us as we made love. Then, when we were satiated, we'd lie face to face, whispering our personal mantra before falling asleep.

"I love you."

"I love you, too."

"Always."

"Forever."

She's at the door again. I don't need to look. She's been there every day and every night since she died.

When the outbreak began, news reports said it was just a variation of seasonal flu. Two days later hospitals were over capacity, the rail network had all but collapsed, and military troops had been deployed to quell riots in major cities. The flu outbreak became an epidemic so fast that it overwhelmed the country. The epidemic turned into an apocalypse; at least according to the last radio transmissions we'd heard five days back. The radio announcer was somewhere in London, he never said where, and when he wasn't quoting from the Bible, or quietly sobbing to himself, he was repeating the same information over and over.

The dead walked.

When I first heard him say that, I thought maybe he was infected; perhaps insanity or delusion was one of the symptoms. But his story didn't change. For two days he reported that the dead were moving, attacking healthy people, tearing them apart.

Devouring them.

We didn't believe it, at first. But then the power died, the phones went dead, and, finally, even the radio went quiet.

Rebecca and I didn't make love that night. The sheets never warmed beneath us. We just held each other, our bodies forming a sanctuary around her swollen stomach as if we could cradle and protect our unborn child with ourselves. Six months earlier we had cried at the news that we had, finally, created life, and now, in the cold, dark night, we cried again.

I had hoped that, living in the middle of Norfolk on an old farm, we'd be safe from the outbreak and the horrors it brought. We were ten miles from the nearest village and only a few hundred people lived there. We were miles and hours away from the nearest city. We would be safe.

The next day Rebecca threw-up. We both smiled thin smiles and pretended it was just a form of morning sickness. She hadn't been sick throughout the whole pregnancy, of course, but maybe she had a price to pay for becoming a mother after all. When a swelling under her armpit started to bleed, however, and a fever set in, we stopped smiling.

I sat with her all that day and through the night. I mopped at her scarlet skin with tepid water and wiped bile and vomit from her mouth. She cried small tears through swollen eyes, and screamed out in pain-fueled incoherency.

And then she stilled.

I rested my hand on her stomach and prayed for movement, any movement. I watched her chest rise and fall, slow and gentle. Exhausted, I leaned my head against her head, ignoring the smell of sickness...

...sunlight streaming through the window pierced my eyes as I woke, and I glanced around the silent bedroom. The sweat-stained sheets were empty. As I staggered to my feet, I caught my reflection in the dresser mirror; the word scrawled there in her favorite lipstick.

"Always."

I stumbled down the stairs and heard a rhythmic thumping coming from beyond the kitchen. I ran through fallen chairs and by the scattered tablecloth before I saw her through the window in the door. Her skin taut and pale, eyes fixed and glassy, she walked into the door time, after time, after time.

I fell to my knees and swallowed the bitter taste of bile. As I had slept in our bed, that final night together, she'd used the last of her strength to stagger from the house, our house, and die alone in the night. She'd known what she would become, what she would've done to me if she'd died in my arms.

I've been sitting in our bedroom, alone, for three days and three nights now, listening as she walks into the door, trying to return home. Return to me.

Enough.

I walk down to the kitchen where moonlight streams in through the glass. I open the door. She moves toward me with a rictus smile of...longing? I see her swollen stomach writhe and my eyes fill. I wait for her embrace.

Whisper, "Forever..."

Jay Faulkner resides in Northern Ireland though home is wherever his loved ones are—his wife, best-friend, and soul mate, Carole, and their two wonderful baby boys, Mackenzie and Nathaniel. While he's a writer, martial artist, sketcher, and dreamer, he's mostly just a husband and father. Jay's short stories have been published widely both online and in print anthologies Jay founded and edits *With Painted Words*, a creative writing site with inspiration from monthly image prompts.

DANCING TONIGHT! LIVE MUSIC!

NATHAN CROWDER

When there was nothing living left to eat, the zombies resumed the patterns of their former lives. Many hadn't been far from being zombies to begin with. With Harold and Joyce, their routine had been dancing at the honky-tonk, and sex.

No music played at Mae's Blue Hollow anymore, but dancers still showed up, shuffling lifelessly through a dead-fall of peanut shells and rotting parts.

Joyce wore her corn-silk yellow dress, the strained cotton clinging to her damp body like it never had in life. Harold wore jeans and an unbuttoned, black western shirt, unselfconsciously displaying the fetid bite on his stomach that had turned him.

Even without the jukebox, they heard the same music, their milky eyes locked on one another. Their jaws were slack, a pantomime of heavy breathing though their lungs no longer drew air.

Harold slid his arms around Joyce's slender waist, pulling her close. His hips ground against hers. His right hand traced her curves. Wandering fingers cupped a pale buttock the same temperature as the Oklahoma prairie outside. Her body responded out of habit, her knee raising, rubbing up the outside of her man's thigh.

Both dancers groaned. There was a hunger that could not be sated in the throaty croak of their voices.

Her ankle curled behind his thigh. He gripped her buttock tighter.

The dance took another, more frenzied note. Others in Mae's Blue Hollow were forgotten. Nothing mattered but the hunger.

Harold's left hand tugged on limp, dark hair, tilting Joyce's head back. A clump of hair came free in his hand, but neither of them noticed. Tight, blue lips found the hollow of her throat, and kissed deeply.

Through the black shirt, Joyce's narrow, talon-like fingers roughly traced well established furrows in Harold's back. She rubbed her pelvis joylessly against the button fly of his jeans. Habit, more than passion drove her. Habit guided her hand down his clammy, bare chest. Habit traced the indentation her teeth had made in his belly. The wound never stopped seeping, tacky to the touch ever since the infection. Her fingers came away damp.

Joyce licked her finger, slowly. Her dry, swollen tongue rasped across sagging skin and sharp bone. She growled, and lowered her swollen lips to his. Tongues met, probed loose teeth in dissolving gums, retracted. The two corpses writhed against each other, wet sounds where skin met skin and parted again.

Harold lifted his partner's other leg around his waist, supporting her weight with both hands beneath her squirming ass cheeks. He took a few steps until Joyce's back met the wall next to the cigarette machine. Out of view of the other disinterested corpses, clumsy fingers fumbled with jeans buttons, baring his sex to the darkened honky-tonk. Joyce raised her skirt, allowing access to her rotting flower.

Drinking Joyce in with his eyes, Harold thrust fruitlessly, his flaccid manhood dangling like a windsock on a calm day. Even here, even now, it was only habit, ritual. No desire drove the two dance partners. It was a blessing in a way. Without beating hearts or working nerve endings, the presence of desire would only lead to frustration. Instead, Harold pantomimed impassioned sex with his partner and she pantomimed her pleasure at the act.

A customary seven minutes later it was over without ever having really begun.

Harold hiked his jeans back over his bony hips, buttoning them tight. Joyce smoothed her skirt back down, glancing coyly about the interior of Mae's as if looking to see who had noticed the clandestine act.

With swollen fingers, Harold brushed her cheek. It was a gentle and reassuring gesture. For the barest of moments, it had the feel of something real, something beyond mere ritual. He hooked her chin with a crooked finger, raised her eyes to his own. His lips met hers again and stayed there, still as a grave for several long moments.

Hand in hand, they left the honky-tonk.

There will be dancing tomorrow.

As long as they both can walk, there will be dancing tomorrow.

Nathan Crowder is a Seattle author with Southwest roots, and has a dark sense of humor and love for the macabre. In addition to his Cobalt City universe of super-hero novels, his work has appeared most recently in the anthologies *Close Encounters of the Urban Kind* and *Crossed Genres: Year One*. His urban sci-fi tale, "Deacon Carter's Last Dime," was selected for the South Notable Stories of 2009 long list.

'TIL DEATH DO
OUR PARTS

KAOLIN IMAGO FIRE

David's screams faded into sobs. He let the lamp drop and sagged into his wife—he couldn't have hit her anyway. He wrapped his arms around her as if nothing were wrong, as if he could protect her against the world. Her teeth scraped against his ribs.

He tried to muster rage against the unfairness of it all, but felt only numb. And then he smelled it: blood. Blood filled his senses. He could smell it, taste it, feel it, a block away, sweaty and running. He pushed Linda away, heading for the door. He wanted that writhing flesh in his mouth.

Linda moaned, and something about it caught his attention; he turned back. She was choking, spasms shaking her body. Her eyes begged...but for what? Forgiveness? Destruction?

She coughed out his flesh.

He wanted to say it was okay, but he couldn't. It wasn't. He shook his head sadly.

Her voice came out raw and wet. "Please..."

He knelt, putting his hand on her bare shoulder, and found himself struggling to form words. "Can't..."

Her flesh was cold, rubbery, just a sack of rotting organs wrapped about her soul. And still he loved her. He kissed her neck, barely feeling it through the thickness in his lips; kissed it again, and she pulled closer.

"David..."

He stroked the side of her face with his palm. She turned into the stroke and took his thumb in her mouth, swirling her tongue slowly around it. Her mouth was still warm with his blood, wet and sticky. David pushed his thumb against her teeth, reveling in that slight pressure. He nipped at her neck, slid his tongue sinuously along it. He scraped the nails of his other hand slowly across her back.

She moaned and clenched her jaw against the base of his thumb. He felt the flesh tear, felt her gently strip it from the bone, felt her sucking it off.

"Linda..."

She looked up into his face with the ragged edge of his thumb sticking out from between her lips, her eyes wide with fear and shame. He kissed her. The familiar texture of his own thumb sent a discordant shiver down his body. His thumb was meat. Thick juices seeped from the stub, smeared across her cheek.

David opened his mouth wider, swirling the thumb around with his tongue. Linda pressed against him, cupping his ass, squeezing into the fullness of contact. She locked her mouth on his, angling her teeth in to reclaim the niblet of flesh. He felt her take the thumb back; a sharp pinch as she got the tip of his tongue as well. He raked clawed fists up both sides of her body, gouging deep with passion. She moaned, fumbling for his belt. He clasped her head and kissed the side of her mouth, her cheek, her jaw, her ear. He'd always loved her ears; the peach-fuzz hair, the delicate lobes. He savored the bite like a fine pancetta.

Blood oozed from their wounds, viscous and slimy where it was fresh, sticky where it had congealed further. He pushed against her and she pushed back, ripping his pants down. He kicked his shoes off, and then his pants, ripped her blouse. Linda shrugged off the remains, raised her skirt.

"David..."

He'd never heard her so husky, so full of need. He wanted to gorge on her breasts, but he held back. His head was full of noise, drowning out the words he wanted.

"Not...right."

"David..."

"Wait."

She looked at him with befuddlement, but he shook his head and shambled away. "Bath."

"David."

"Get bath. Wait."

Linda would set out candles, like she always did. He had one thing more to get. Shuffling one foot and then the other forward, he headed to the garage...and slammed into the door, unsure as to why it didn't move. He slammed it again, inertia warring with awareness. He wanted in.

Linda's voice trailed in from the master bathroom, slurring his name. "David?"

"Door!" he screamed.

"Handle, David. Use handle."

He looked down, a vague memory of how to use a door tickling his arm. The door opened and he stumbled into gray darkness. His eyes adjusted until the walls glowed dull red, pulsing with his movements. He grasped the gas can from under the shelving by the door, his hands like fleshy pods at the end of long, cumbersome sticks, then pushed back through the door, towards his love.

Small flames danced at the ends of thick candles arrayed around the edge of the tub. Linda lay in the tub, legs spread, playing with herself idly. Gouges pockmarked her body, and her blood smeared the tub, walls, and curtains. One candle, unlit, was embedded deep in her left thigh.

Closer to her, David felt some of his control, his self, return. He wrenched the cap off the gas can and upended it, dousing himself first, then her.

She looked up at him, eyes unnaturally wide, an expression of peace or lust on her face; a bead of blood trickled slowly down her cheek. "Love...you...David."

He smiled and stepped into the tub, then lay down somewhat uncomfortably beside her. Linda wrapped her legs around him and grabbed him. He reached around to support himself on the ledge of the tub, then pressed his hips forward, letting her guide him in. They worked slowly against each other, seeking a rhythm. Then harder, faster, trying to find one last climax.

Flames licked at David's feet. Gasoline wafted off their bodies, teasing the fire.

And the world exploded.

Kaolin Imago Fire is a conglomeration of ideas, side projects, and experiments. Outside of his primary occupation, he also develops computer games, edits *GUD Magazine*, and very occasionally teaches computer science. He has had short fiction published in *Strange Horizons*, *Bull Spec*, and *Crossed Genres*, among others.

tHERE'S PLENTY OF ROOM IN MY HEART

ALEX MASTERSON

Bone and gristle
Wet my whistle
And nothing makes me hornier
Than gazing into the bloodshot depths
Of my love's shattered cornea
I've never heard a hotter sound
Than when she first crawled out the ground
Her throat let loose a charming belch
Followed by a gentle squelch
And then she moaned through a mouthful of slime
The same groan that still gets me, time after time
She was naked and gray, and covered with ants
Now something else was rising, down in my pants
Later, back home, my dad stared in confusion
"Get her to hospital for a blood transfusion!"
I had to explain seven times that she's dead
Before it finally sunk into his head
She's never been high in my folks' estimation
They scream, and cry, "She's an abomination!"
Just 'cause she tried to devour their cat
They chased her with pitchforks—now how rude is that?
And just because her little heart isn't beating
People presume our relationship's fleeting
But they would think differently if they had seen
The glistening beauty of her perfect spleen
Yes, she might dribble a bit when she talks
And tends to shamble about when she walks
But her mannerisms are just so endearing
Especially now that the graverot is clearing

While running my hand through her dry hair
I sometimes happen upon maggots in there
I'll show her my find and we both share a giggle
And make bets on how far the li'l guys can wriggle
At least, I think that it's mirth which is flowing
It's hard to tell, when half her jawbone is showing
But there is a sparkling deep in her eye
That is so much more than a few nesting flies
I do admit it can get tough
Our sex life is definitely rough
I honestly don't mind the odd bite or two
I just wish she wouldn't then start to chew
I know every couple has their own quirks
And there's no manual to say how love works
But me and my sweetheart are doing just swell
I'm glad that there was no more room left in Hell

Alex Masterson would like to talk a little bit about himself, but the last time he did, his psychiatrist chased him out of the building with a stapler.

LIKE SMOKE

JOHANN CARLISLE

When he is done singing and collapses on the marble stele, I watch the rapid rise and fall of his chest for a while, enjoying the sheen of sweat on his bare skin, his breath like smoke in the moonlight. I itch to touch, to taste his salt, to breathe his sour musk, but I don't yet dare. I don't know if he's ready.

I think back to how his hands, so warm always, coaxed me, teased me, coached me, took what was cold and slack and tickled it to sizzling, oozing life. I close my eyes at the memory, wanting him to break into me all over again, to open me and taste me like he used to when we were both hot and healthy with breathing pores and beating hearts.

But then there was the hospital. I remember nothing after that.

He always liked to play in the dark. It is dark now, but a cold, lonely kind of dark, a dank darkness with hollow winds whistling through monumental stone sentinels. My memorial among them, my earthy bed torn up by his hands.

Not here the bedroom smoke of beeswax and hashish, but the tang of stronger drugs, tallow candles and spices, his midnight offerings of rose oil, gifts of chili and molasses spirit, sacred vévés of cornflour and charcoal. The barbecue smell of charred fresh chicken, and the deeper stink of things longer dead, the corruption that no amount of ginger, allspice and garlic can hide.

Smells, tastes, smoke, the dark. So many stimuli that would normally provoke hunger, thirst, slumber, excitement, but tonight all I can feel is lust for him, lying on the stone slab, his body slowly cooling in the night breeze.

"Pierre," I whisper, stepping forward and scoring my nails gently down his flat, goose-pimpled belly. He shudders softly under my touch, but still doesn't move. I kneel, getting mud on my Sunday best, reach for the snakeskin belt holding up his linen pants. The smell of him does the trick.

I almost whimper as I flick my tongue against the end of his flaccid cock a few times, then as he starts to stiffen, I take it into my mouth, moisten it with my tongue, and swallow.

Pierre stirs now. First he gasps audibly, then a cough that might have been my name or the word "Dieu." His hands grope weakly at my shoulders, then fingers tangle in my hair and he clutches me to him, a shudder starting in his throat like he's about to sing an *pryie*.

In return I tug at his pants, pulling them down and caressing with both hands the slack skin of his sinewy legs. I don't try to pull the pants over his cowboy boots, instead I move my hands back to his hips, cup his buttocks, knead them, dig in my fingers and open his ass. All the time I am working over his slick cock, the smell of him almost overpowering me.

When finally his come gushes into my throat like watery soup, I swallow and swallow and swallow. There is no temptation to choke or spit, I just want my man inside me. He is softening again before I let him go.

Pierre sits up to face me as I perch on the edge of the stele beside him. He leans close to look into my face, and in the glow of dying coals I see his eyes are already starting to turn milky.

The marks made by my fingers are still there, little holes in his flesh, not springing back like they would on a healthy body.

"What did this cost you, Pierre?" I ask.

He gasps the first time he tries to speak. I hold him steady. He tries again.

"No more than it was worth," he says hoarsely. "I couldn't live without you."

Before I can protest he kisses me, and suddenly our tongues are probing, licking at yellow teeth and drying gums, sucking with chapped lips and breathing each other's stale breath with lungs slowly filling with mucus. Both our lives dissipating like smoke. We hold each other for a long time. Then I pull away.

"Let me get you home, Pierre," I say with a smile. "You look like shit."

"Heh," he chuckles. "Look who's talking. You look like death warmed over."

He pulls up his pants, and we leave the cemetery to head back to the French Quarter where Pierre has a small apartment.

We probably don't have long. We'll make it count.

Johann Carlisle is a Machiavellian illusion created to serve as the corporeal avatar of a sentient artificial intelligence that may or may not be of terrestrial origin. He is being watched. His short fiction has been published in markets such as *The Future Fire*, *Black Petals*, *The Harrow*, and *Sein und Werden*.

SURRENDER

XANDER BRIGGS

Liv had eaten the last of the food two days ago, and now her hunger was so constant she barely felt it, just another dull ache in her belly to join the ones in her head and heart. She was tired.

She lived on the couch now, in her childlike pillow-fortress with blankets and books and candle (just one left) within reach, and the pot in the corner she'd been using since the plumbing stopped. She knew she should retreat further into the apartment, put more doors between herself and the hall, but for some reason, that scared her more. She wanted to be here, where she could hear them moving. Where she could see her death coming before it struck.

It was evening, and the creatures outside were beginning to howl.

She rested her cheek on the arm of the sofa and stared at the door. Everything had gone wrong at once. She'd gone out drinking with her girlfriends, come home, and fought with James. She'd said things she hadn't meant, threw a pile of his clothes into the hall, and he'd just shook his head and left. At the time, she'd thought that he didn't care, but maybe he was just being logical, level-headed, James. Now he was gone, and she was alone, and kept getting his voicemail when she tried to call him. The world had ended, and the irrational voice in the back of her head told her it was her fault.

There was a louder howl, closer... In the building? As far as she knew, the other tenants were gone. Dead or wandering. Another howl, questioning, questing, close. Close as they'd been in days.

Weeks? They blurred together. Footsteps, now. Down the hall? She lifted her head, cupped her hand to her ear. She heard the steps clearly, slow and heavy, the ragged breaths. Then she heard it stop, snuffling, growling... It was strange. They weren't quite animal noises. She could tell they came from a human throat, changed as it was.

It hit the door with a violent bang that seemed to shake the apartment. She heard it shuffle away a few steps, and had time to wonder if it had given up, before WHAM! Step, step, WHAM! Again. Pictures rattled on the walls.

Her eyes scanned the room quickly, landed on the table. She could push it over, in front of the door, buy herself time...

No, a voice in her mind whispered. *You're weak and tired. You're dying, and everyone's gone. James is gone. What's the point in fighting?*

What was the point?

A little laugh bubbled up her throat and she was on her feet, stumbling, falling to her knees, then up again and moving. How long had it been since she'd walked? She was moving more clumsily than one of *them*. The thought made her laugh again, and she was laughing still as she got to the door, as she unlocked it, and only stopped when she realized the creature had fallen silent.

She opened the door and stared into its face.

Oh.

Of course.

James stood hunched and bloody in the doorway. He was nearly naked, shirtless, jeans and boxers hanging in tatters from the waistband, making it easy for her to see the pale and purple-veined expanse of his flesh, the way his muscles seemed to twitch and writhe of their own accord. His clawed hands. His sunken stomach. She thought she saw movement from beneath his still-buckled belt, but the scraps and shadows hid that part of him.

His eyes were glassy, but focused. His lips parted, revealing jagged teeth, and his tongue flicked in the dark.

"Luh," he said. "Luhf."

She couldn't tell if he was saying her name, or something else; couldn't bear to think about it, so she didn't reply at all, just reached out to lay a hand on his chest.

It wasn't as cold as she'd expected.

"Luhf," he repeated.

"James?" she asked.

"Need," he answered, and lifted a gnarled hand toward her face.

She brushed his fingertips with her own.

Then he pounced.

He was stronger than he had ever been in life; he who had played varsity football and lifted weights three times a week. He shoved her insistently down, claw-like hands pinning her shoulders, knees somehow ending up between hers. His breath was on her face and his eyes were on hers and she heard the sound of tearing cloth but realized through a haze that she wasn't scared. Shouldn't she be?

But he was on her, and he was her James again, and his mouth was covering her breast, and there was a pinprick sharpness around her areola before the cold tongue found her nipple and drove the thought away. She gasped, a surge of arousal flooding through her. Then the cool mouth was hot and wet, and she opened her eyes to see his face, and her chest wet with blood, and she had the giddy thought that it didn't hurt. None of it hurt after the first bite. He was licking her stomach—at least, she thought it was licking—and if she closed her eyes she could forget that it was anything but good.

Her hips, her thighs, her—Oh! That wasn't a tongue—but it was good, so good! And as she felt him kiss her neck, her last thoughts were joyful, that he had come back for her, wanted her, and she surrendered herself to him as darkness rose in an orgasmic crescendo.

Liv howled.

Xander Briggs lives and writes in the Florida panhandle, where he is absolutely prepared in case of an undead uprising.

I FALL TO PIECES

EDWARD MORRIS

At some point, we all fail, and wander thereafter like a zombie too stupid to realize it's shambling around losing body parts.

Sometimes, it's better to remember them the way they were.

# # #

No one would understand out here, on Christmas Eve. People are merry and drunk everywhere. I can't be here...

# # #

The summer I was seventeen, five sweltering weeks on an old college campus, I fell in love with a beautiful freak named Spektra Triantafelakis. She was in the Poetry thesis at Governor's Honors, I was Fiction. We made a lot of plans, like going to colleges two miles apart. She wanted us to get a place and work and drink and write and paint and screw and...

Back when I was new in Philly, I remember that look on her face, like she couldn't stop smiling when I was there. Through Philly.com, buried in the years before, I found Spek's obituary last month.

I think I can miss her, now.

I do.

# # #

It's snowing. Trying to look sober enough to sneak in the door, order some food and coffee to lay on top of this drunk, and...

Aw, hell.

I remember that Christmas Eve when I met up with Spektra in the blue dawn outside her apartment on Tasker Street. I remember the way her cheeks colored in the cold; that look...

I remember biting her lower lip gently, sucking on it. I remember the sounds she made. I remember her firm, round breasts, warm against my ribs as she rucked off my black hoodie. I remember the way her thighs gripped my hipbones hard enough to bruise. I remember the mythic heat of her warm flesh, the fluttering muscles of her flat belly.

I remember the way her hot, slithery cunt swallowed me whole and how time vaporized on our first real Christmas morning after. We fell asleep entwined, and rolled over warm to entwine every way again until the sun was up and shining off the snow that was going, but leaving some of itself behind.

# # #

1435 Tasker St. Unit #1109. CIESLAK, NIKOLAS G., HELD FOR QUESTIONING IN OVERDOSE DEATH. UNIDENTIFIED FEMALE — D.O.A., AGE 30 APPROX.

# # #

"The new boi's name is Nick Cieslak. He makes movies. He's coming over. We shot one the other night. 'f I tell you something, do you promise..."

"Yeah, sure, whatever. What'd you take?" I was already tired of the pre-Renaissance form of torture known as "Just Friends."

"A little bit of cheap black tar heroin. Nothing big. The cheaper it is, the weaker it is... You wanna see what we shot?"

I had to think for a long time before answering. I left mid-way through a home movie mostly featuring naked Spek nodded out on heroin in the bathtub.

After my third pitcher of beer, I was politely ejected from Fergie's Pub. They were cool about it. I just went home and slept it off.

# # #

At seven-thirty tonight, I got this phone call.

"Ed-ward Mor-ris." Spek sounded strange. "You'll never guess where I'm calling from..."

I had to sit down on the curb. "This is sick. This is Christmas Eve. You're dead. I don't mean that, like, but...kid, you died. How..."

I popped the flask from my trench coat pocket. "Where's Nick?"

"Graterford. For murder. He...let...someone...overdose. Anyway, I'm at the Barber Theatre on Broad and Main. We need to talk."

"Okay, but—"

CLICK.

I finished the whiskey. It wasn't helping. I knew the theater. It wasn't far from the crenellated stone atrium of City Hall, where they filmed "Twelve Monkeys" the year we broke up...

I don't even remember taking the Orange line down there. But I remember getting off, and walking up out onto the street.

# # #

Everything looked timeless, in the beauty of a Philadelphia snowstorm, as the Spek-thing shambled toward me from the dark lot behind the movie-house, leaving loopy herringbone tracks like a wounded animal.

The broken marionette showed no fear of the few people or cars in evidence. She flung small pieces of herself, when she supplicated with those bare, rotten hands. She still had that high pair of black boots. One of them was on backwards. One of her legs, one of her blue legs, was twisted so that it looked like it was...

Every stored-up last word evaporated. The wind rose, stealing my breath for its own. I was pretty sure I'd only ever smell her again. I realized I had a cigarette lit in both my hands. One for each of us. That pulled her up short.

"You ask too much of people," she croaked, but swiped one of the cigarettes from my hand. "People will always let you down." If I just kept eye contact, I could concentrate. Mostly. She was looking at me like I was the one falling apart.

"Just because something doesn't work forever doesn't mean it wasn't special, shouldn't be valued—"

"Did you come back just to flip me shit?" I asked.

Spek looked up into my eyes, and reached her tiny, skinned hand for mine.

I had her head off in one clean twist.

# # #

There was a group of drunks shambling down the street that didn't stop to look. There was a dumpster around the corner. None of the removal and disposal took very long.

# # #

There's a steak on the way. Black coffee in front of me. Fergie accepted my apology; said he'd already forgotten. But no more booze for a while. Rest...and maybe waking, someday.

Maybe resurrection.

I think I can miss Spek, now that I killed her again.

I do.

Edward Morris is a 2005 BSFA nominee, also nominated for the 2009 Rhysling. His work has appeared in *Interzone, Helix, Arkham Tales* and many other publications worldwide. His series, *There Was a Crooked Man,* was released from Mercury Retrograde Press fall 2010.

UNPARTED

WENDY N. WAGNER

He plunges inside her with a squelch of leaking fluids. There are no tight muscles to squeeze his penis, but the sloshing movement of loose organs against him is more intense than a blow job. His wife was always amazing in bed. She hasn't lost her touch after death.

She can't moan, but she pulls him in deeper and harder than she could before, before even yesterday, when her cervix gave way and he found himself inside her cold womb. Beyond this point, there is an even newer intimacy. He gasps, thrusts twice into her intestinal folds. They twist around him, sticking, caressing like the tenderest of tongues. He calls her name as he comes.

His own living liquids blend with the yellow slurry of her innards, spilling out over the rubber sheet.

He holds her tightly in his arms, burying his nose in the still-soft threads of her hair. Four years ago, a sinus infection

claimed his sense of smell. He can still remember the sweet apple scent of her favorite shampoo; it's what he smells now inside his mind.

"I love you," he whispers.

She taps her forehead gently against his collarbone. Without lung function, there is no way for her to speak. This is their code, one tap for "yes," two for "no." It is nothing like the conversations they had when she was alive, whole nights floating past on a current of words. But it is better than the loneliness of no words at all.

She rolls over and spoons against him. He kisses her neck and resists the urge to pick at the strip of skin peeling away from her shoulder. It's not easy—he is a picker by nature, a popper of pimples, a scratcher of scabs—but he restrains himself. He wants her to last as long as possible.

He brushes his finger over her cheek. "Don't leave me," he murmurs, just as he's pleaded every day since she came home with the biopsy results. "Please don't leave me."

She taps the back of her head twice against his chest, as solemn a promise as their wedding vows.

Wendy N. Wagner's short fiction is forthcoming in *Beneath Ceaseless Skies*, and has appeared in *Crossed Genres* and *The Way of the Wizard* anthology. Her poetry has appeared in *Abyss and Apex*. She is the Assistant Editor of Fantasy Magazine, and lives in Portland, Oregon, with her very understanding family—and no zombies.

RETURNED

J. R. CAMPBELL

She was deaf to the familiar, the thunder of wave against stone, the howling of the night winds, but the thud of his feet as he staggered up the wooden steps shocked her awake. He was coming for her. Again. Rosalind squeezed her lids over eyes raw from weeping and tried to still the trembling of her limbs. Flight was impossible; like everything else she had loved, any chance of escape had disappeared beneath the waves. Dreading his approach, uncertain she could endure another night, Rosalind buried her face in a pillow and pulled the covers over her head, grateful for the bit of warmth separating her from her drowned husband.

He would climb the stairs with agonizing slowness, each shambling step a defiance of death. When he reached her door he would pause as if he still had breath to catch and then—just as she was certain the blow would never fall—he would bang his fist against the wooden barrier.

For hours he would hammer, begging entrance. Rosalind lay huddled in her bed, shaking and weeping until sometime before dawn when he turned and thudded slowly down the wooden steps and—with a horrible splash—vanished beneath the waves again. Where did he go after that? Did he walk on the seafloor where his nets had dragged him under? Did he float like a wraith among the creatures of the deep? Did he wait in the mouth of the harbor, looking up at the surface he'd once rowed her across? Such imaginings threatened to tear her mind apart. Worst of all was when she saw them all together, broken bones entangled, tendrils of rotting flesh intermingled, a flash of gold winking like betrayal. All Rosalind had loved, now bashed and battered together by the relentless tide. Tumbling corpses welcoming her husband as they were thrown back and forth like stones on a beach.

Her parents would be there. Rosalind had precious few memories of them; her father's mischievous smile, the warmth of her mother's embrace. They'd tried to escape, waiting only until their daughter was old enough to travel. Mostly Rosalind remembered bobbing up and down in the frigid waves, the long faces of the men who had pulled her into their little boat, the merciless stars glimpsed through a hole in the storm clouds. They'd returned her to the island and presented her to her mother's sister.

"Our family is cursed," Aunt Lillian explained. "Unless we escape, the sea will take us both."

But how to escape an island without challenging the ocean? Lillian claimed she knew. It was possible, Lillian assured her, but they needed gold to hold the magic. It would take time. Until the enchantment was finished Rosalind was forbidden to walk on the shore or sit in a boat, even one pulled safely ashore.

And then there was Ervin, who'd never been afraid of the sea. The boy had always been there, almost as if he were waiting— but, such thoughts were foolish. Still, she and Ervin had always known they belonged together. As season followed season they circled each other, drawn together by a force neither understood.

One summer afternoon Rosalind had climbed along a wooded ridge overlooking the bit of shoreline where Ervin worked on his boat. She'd spent the afternoon watching him as he shaved down the hull, thin wooden peelings sticking to his bare arms and chest as he labored. Only when the shadows started to lengthen, did Rosalind head back to her aunt's house, but Lillian had intercepted her on the hillside.

"It's done," Lillian said without preamble.

"What is?" Rosalind asked.

Aunt Lillian held out her hand, opening her fist to reveal gold. "The charm. It's finished. Here." Lillian pressed the warm metal into Rosalind's hand. "Hold it tight," her aunt urged. "Close your eyes and wish as hard as you can to be somewhere safe. When you open your eyes again you will be far from the sea, among people who have never heard the crash of the waves or known the taste of saltwater. There, you'll be safe. Do it now."

Rosalind paused, then shook her head.

Anger and frustration touched Lillian's face. "You know what will happen if you don't. Go on."

"What about you?" Rosalind asked.

"There isn't enough gold for two," Lillian said. "Don't worry about—"

"No." Rosalind said. "I won't leave you."

It wasn't, Rosalind could see, a thought that had ever occurred to her aunt. Lillian's look of surprise faded as tears threatened to spill from her eyes. Lillian pulled her niece close.

"Well," she said. "I suppose you needn't leave just yet. Just promise me you'll always keep it with you."

Rosalind lived with her aunt through that winter. When the sea-ice melted Lillian started to look disapprovingly at Ervin, sensing that he might be part of the reason Rosalind had put off her escape. The days grew longer and then shorter. Before spring could come again Lillian fell through the ice walking home from her sister's grave marker. Careless. The sea returned no trace of her.

In the spring they carved a marker for Lillian and placed it next to her sister's. The gold charm was warm in her hand as Rosalind pondered escape. But Ervin was there, beside her.

They married the following spring. Custom insisted the husband row his new bride across the harbor's calm water. Rosalind had been terrified, her frantic movements rocking the tiny craft, but Ervin took her across quickly and safely. If she hadn't been so frightened she might not have dropped the charm in the sea. A loss, but she had crossed the waves safely. Perhaps the curse was broken.

# # #

Ervin's cold fist hammered on the door. In her bed Rosalind squeezed her eyes closed and wished as fiercely as she could to be somewhere far away. Nothing happened, of course. What would he do if she opened the door? Ervin had always been generous with his love; did he seek one final embrace? Rosalind trembled under her covers, imagining his cold, wet touch. The curse drove him, she was sure of it, mocking the love they'd shared. There was no escape.

Finally Ervin's desperate hammering rattled her mind to the point where something shifted. Rosalind pulled down the covers. If she didn't rise now she never would again; the knife beside her bed would see to that. Slowly, deliberately, she lowered her bare feet to the floor and stood. She sought a robe, something to wear over her thin shift, felt the press of hysterical laughter. As if a robe would help.

Despair crashed against her like waves against worn rock. The door shook in its frame as Ervin banged ever harder against the wood. With steps smaller than a child's she inched slowly toward the door. She closed her eyes.

The hammering stopped. When Rosalind looked again, she saw her hand on the knob. She'd opened it.

Rosalind felt her newfound determination sag as the sight of Ervin wrenched her anew. His gray, bloated body; the seawater dripping from hair and clothes; empty sockets where bright eyes should have been; a face no longer capable of expression. His rotting form was forlorn; wretched beyond hope of redemption. He stood motionless, his left hand raised, ready to resume his hammering.

"Ervin—" his name escaped her lips.

The corpse trembled at the whispered sound of his name. His left arm fell. In a jerky motion he raised his other hand, reaching towards her. She cringed, stepping back despite her resolve.

The touch she dreaded didn't come. Ervin's outstretched hand was open. On his palm a piece of gold—untouched by the sea's cruelty—glittered in the starlight.

Shaking, she reached for the lost charm; gasped as her fingers brushed the soft, cold flesh of his hand. But the gold warmed quickly to her touch, its weight familiar.

"Thank you," she whispered, but he had already turned back to the sea.

J. R. Campbell's works have appeared in a variety of magazines, anthologies, and on radio's *Imagination Theater*. The works he would most like to direct your attention to are W. H. Horner's *Fantastical Visions IV* and the Gaslight books: *Gaslight Grimoire: Fantastic Tales of Sherlock Holmes* and *Gaslight Grotesque: Nightmare Tales of Sherlock Holmes*. He is currently co-editing a third collection of Sherlock Holmes stories with his friend, Charles Prepolec.

REVENGE

LOVE, LOVE (AND CHAINS) WILL KEEP US TOGETHER...

R. SCHUYLER DEVIN

A convergence of misfortune is what they called the great extinction of life. It wasn't an extinction of physical form, but, rather, the essence of life: higher reasoning, ingenuity, spirituality, and accountability. Most of the living are now dead—robbed of life, but not motivity. A convergence of designer neurochemical enhancers—slurped down in sugary carbonated tonics more popular than the "bull" and "superstar" energy drinks ever were—reacting in the limbic system with a microbe that hitched a ride on a rock brought back from Jupiter's moon, Ganymede. Scientists say that if our bodies hadn't been pumped full of love potions and cognitive enhancers, our first contact with an extraterrestrial life form would've left us with only prolonged headaches and an aggressive pox. Humanity had made its own bed to be screwed in: figuratively and literally.

The "Thrax," as it's called (short for "thrusting attack"), wasn't immediately fatal. It was like tossing gasoline on the sexual fire burning in the paleomammalian part of the brain. If you combined the worst parts of a serial rapist, a crack addict, and an obsessive-compulsive, you'd understand the typical infectee. When the infected began dying, and *still* didn't stop violating the masses, shit got dead serious.

Most thought the world was ending, and doomsayers wagged their fingers in vindication, but when Becky came bursting though my door—no, really, all one hundred and thirty pounds of her splintered my apartment door off its hinges—I saw the Thrax as a new beginning. I'll admit, at first I was scared. Who wouldn't be if the girl of your dreams—the girl you ordered coffee from every day for two years (though you hate coffee, and watched her smile at every guy but you)—broke down your door to find you watching the scrambled Skin-a-max channel, contemplating if it was worth getting up to grab the lotion? It was only of mild concern that she was missing the fingers from both hands and smelled of rancid bacon fat poured down a New Delhi storm drain. I couldn't believe it: Becky was in my flat, wearing torn next-to-nothings. The fact that she was dead, and still didn't favor me with a smile, was only a mere technicality in our love connection. My guidance counselor was right when he'd suggested I'd make a good mortician, but it probably would've lead to a string of heartbreaks.

My first instinct was flight when she leapt from the threshold and cleared my couch with ease; then I remembered how much I wanted her, and relaxed my defenses. I could still hear the timbre of her voice within the growling, and imagined she was professing her love for me but just couldn't find the right words. I wanted this—what guy doesn't want to be screwed to death?—but in this instance, actual death could be involved. I needed to play it safe. I held my hand out like I used to when my mastiff was agitated. I said everything was fine. Told her that she need not force it, I'd participate willingly. She slowed her advance—could she understand me? I backed up to my patio door, opened the screen, and crouched down to grab my dog's old collar and chain. Told her to follow me as I skirted around towards the bedroom, and she obeyed. I pulled my shorts down and jumped onto the bed, bouncing a few times like an excited kid about to get a surprise. I ripped my shirt off—seriously, I've always wanted to—and commanded she take me. Again, she crossed the distance in one unnatural bound, and was on me before I could take a mental snapshot of the moment. I screamed in pain, thinking she was going to tear it off, but she responded by lessening the assault. I was sure she could understand me.

The smell of her—the sweet rot—unsettled my stomach along with the butterflies; that clenching and fluttering of new love churning, black winged, feasting on the love of the dead. Unless you've ever loved a decaying angel, you could never understand such necrotic pleasure. I reached over to the nightstand drawer and felt around for my handcuffs. I might have been a virgin, but I was a hopeful virgin, prepared for fantasy. Reaching up, I clasped the dog collar around Becky's neck and she didn't protest, caught up in single-minded action like a cowhand breaking in a saddle. I placed one end of the handcuffs through links in the chain leash and locked it, and placed the other end around one of the bars of my bed frame.

It was my turn as I hoisted her off me and threw her onto the bed. Every push, every thrust, was a path to heaven while driving through the gates of hell. She moaned—pleasure? I swear it was different from the groaning; that she loved me and not just as a tool to fulfill a primal need. A vital release at the peak of bliss and crescendo left me spent and shuttering. We made love countless times over lost days and I kept her trussed to the bed, though I believe she stayed willingly. I wouldn't risk losing her now that she was mine; the Thrax might've driven her into another's arms.

Weeks passed and she improved with smiles and partial words. I washed her skin and gray decay flaked off. Eight semesters of biology and two university visits confirmed my hunch: Becky was not dead but on the verge of death—as many infectees are now thought to be—and my body contained antibodies that might be key to ending the alien doomsday. I transmitted these antibodies to her, and somehow they survived her compromised immune system.

I arrive home to tell Becky the news. She's now more than just a shadow of her former beauty and implores me to let her go, but I can't, we're meant to be together. Reaching for the chain around her neck, she's reminded she has no fingers to facilitate escape; is destined to be a captive of love. She'd be one of the mindless dead if fate had not joined us, and I fear she'll flee forever when she discovers that, within this dream, *I'm* the real monster.

R. Schuyler Devin prefers to walk the halls of his own imagining rather than the dark alleyways of his past. He's a writer, musician, and brazen geek, who lives under the silver skies of Washington State with his tireless wife and dynamic daughter.

ERZULI'S CHOSEN FEW

LUCIA STARKEY

He kept his head shaved smooth, against the blistering heat of August. On its shiny surface I saw every dream and hope of love I'd ever had. His hands were strong from hauling crates from ship to dock and back again. And those arms, those thighs; I knew their firm, silken feel before I ever held him close in the humid dark of that long, late summer.

My mama was a mambo, a good witch with great power. When we married, my mama said a prayer over us, the scent of sticky red blood barely noticeable over the stinking sweat of our bodies. I felt blessed to be having that man for my own; thought for sure I was one of Erzuli's chosen few. And Erzuli, that goddess of love, she laughed at me.

When winter came, and the work stopped, that's when things changed. What had once been tenderness and honey between us became bitter and rough. Late at night, with my hand on my privates, aching from his wrath, I let sticky tears run like blood onto my pillow.

Spring came. Back at work, he'd smile and his walk became easy again, but in the dark I still feared the stirrings of his punishing cock. Blacker than the dark, he'd rise above me, thrusting against raw pain that never had time to heal. And Erzuli laughed because still, I loved him.

My mama was a mambo, a good witch, so it wasn't hers to give, what I needed. I found a bokor, with a dry voice like bones against linen and a different set of gifts.

I went to the dock that last day, that first day. I watched my tall, handsome man as he joked with his friends. His head was shaved again, but the only reflection was the sun. His teeth flashed white, but disappeared when he saw me. When did that happen? I wondered. When did the guilt enter his eyes?

When the workers broke in the middle of the day to rest and eat, I took his hand in mine and we walked home, quiet. I had a rooster in the kitchen, one leg tied to the table; it was the rooster's throat I meant to cut.

Sticky red, too much for a cup, so I caught it in the wash tub. Out of the sun, the shine of his head was muted, soft, and I held it to my chest as the cut drained. Then, because he scared me still, I used my knife again and put his manhood in a jar, safe in the back of the pantry.

But you see, I loved him, and there's no "death do ye part" where my mamma's bindings lie. I used the bokor's words to set my love against Baron Samedi, and dared him to take my man from me.

Day melted into dark, and in the dusk between, I caught my love's *bon ange*, and held tight. Without a proper grave to guard, the black Baron's grasp was weak. "Here," I told him, "take the little bit my lover doesn't need, but let me keep his greater soul, for I have need of that." With all my force of love and strength, I pulled my darling's soul from Death. Erzuli's laughter grew.

Smooth and firm, from the stitched line at his throat to the one near his legs, my beautiful love. Fear gone, I went to him and took him in my arms. We made love that night. Without the urgency of his cock, my man was sweet and tender; the joy of being with him came through me, soft and warm as blood.

Those hands, rough from work, hummed along my skin. That mouth, full of whispered apologies and honey kisses, found every longing curve. When dawn came, the subtle light reflected off his smooth shaved head, and once again, I saw my dreams.

The men at the dock no longer joked with my husband. They gave him a wide berth and some made the sign of a hex behind his back. But when he turned to me and flashed his white smile, I didn't care what they thought at all.

Winter came again. We spent our days in bed, murmuring sweet nothings through short days, moaning nothing-at-alls through long nights. Then one day something inside me shifted and I wanted more.

"I need him all," I said. "I need the part you took."

But Baron Samedi couldn't give it back.

My cuts and stitches held my husband's flesh tight, no space for the *ti bon ange*. The Baron offered back that little piece of soul, but with no flesh to house it, it couldn't come home. Unless...

A cock for a cock, that's what I paid. And as Baron Samedi drank, sticky red, and the rooster twitched and died, I stitched and sewed, giving back what I had taken, so the little soul could take root again. When the Baron was done, he smiled at me, red over white in his dark face. Then he laughed, joining Erzuli in her joke.

My love was not patient with me that night. It had been a long time for him, and though he screamed in pain as his sex pulled taut against my needlework, he made sure I screamed along.

It's a funny thing. A soul, once ripped from flesh, doesn't hold as strong. In that flash of pleasure and pain, as my love loosed his seed in my punished depths, his fragile *bon ange* loosed as well.

My son works the docks, some days I go to watch him. He keeps his head shaved smooth, against the blistering heat of August. On its shiny surface, I can see every memory of love I've ever known.

Lucia Starkey was born yesterday and died October 16, 2004. None of this helped with writing zombie erotica, though death has given her an interesting perspective on romance. "Erzuli's Chosen Few" will be her first published story, and Lucia would like to thank all the writers and editors who made this collection possible.

YOUR BEATING HEART

M. G. GILLETT

He was a risk taker and thrill maker. He loved himself and gambled it all; had faith enough to wait.

Oh, how he *trusted* you.

You would save him, if he climbed too deep or stayed too long; became pinned alone in the blackness of a cave. He trusted you, waited for you, ached for you.

He was a hunter, seeking stories of adrenaline for your after-dinner delight. Those adventures that hide 'round the next crushing corner and end coiled in your intoxicating arms. But this time, in his haste to go deeper, become harder, fate finally took him.

But not fast, mind. These cursed things often take time.

Think about it—and please, help yourself. Another cheese? Some pâté?

He would've known he was trapped. Can you feel with him the cold stone at your back, each breath coming sharper than the last as the earth constricts, blackness drifting in as you lie wedged between rock and Hell?

For a while he would've known with comforting certainty that you'd come for him. Known in his heart he was a fool, but that the righteous would risk all to save a fool. As he died, the final insight into your heart would've struck him like an electric bolt.

You were never righteous.

You didn't come.

And now he hears the ancient call, rises dutifully from his consecrated grave, the worldly pounding of wet, beating hearts beckoning.

And he seeks you.

Why? you ask.

So you know how it *feels*.

Can you possibly imagine? To awaken underground, the crushing weight of earth pinning your arms and legs, your eyes pushed deep in your skull, your mouth full of the black dirt of your own grave.

Oh, don't upset yourself so.

These melancholy tombs are all alike. Wet clay or rich loam—the dead have tasted it all.

You will taste it too, one day.

Think now. And have another glass of wine. You're looking flushed.

Imagine what must've gone through his mind as first a finger, then a knuckle, then a hand clenched and clutched and strained to pick free of the prison in which you put him. *You* put him, or so he understands.

It's only hunger now that sustains him. Hunger for those that live on to disappoint the dead.

Will you disappoint him again, when he finds you?

He's coughed out the dirt—not a cough of air, but a spasmodic heaving retch to cleanse himself of the last of the black earth.

It took only a moment to understand. Never another breath to take. Only hunger remains. And now he follows the luscious scent of your warm and throbbing heart.

Oh! You spilled your wine. You might want to change.

But not yet. Consider.

Have you silently thanked your God it was him instead of you? They broke his bones to get him out you know. His body had bloated obscenely in death. The torpid shell that remains is nothing like the hard body you knew; his firm, young flesh now hanging loose in tatters, the night crawlers having satisfied their own needs.

But he still has teeth, and is still, very much, a man.

How do you feel? Are you aroused?

He'd know that scent.

Or—do you reek of fear? Because, you know, that only hardens his appetite. He loves that game.

His touch will be rough. Prepare now. Make peace with your conscience.

Good night.

Sleep tight.

He follows your heartbeat, don't fight.

M. G. Gillett is a Calgary writer and this is his first publication, though he's won and placed several times in short story competitions held in Calgary. He loves the idea of a Canadian style of writing—not to imply that Canadians prefer the dead as their medium, but that Canada has some real living talent with amazing original ideas.

BREATHING OPTIONAL

KAY T. HOLT

In spite of all evidence to the contrary, Elena wasn't dead. Sure, she didn't have a heartbeat and breathing was optional, but she was still very much...hungry. Now, there was a word for Elena. And, like the stereotype, she hungered for one thing in particular: brains. She wouldn't turn up her nose at a nice piece of ass, though.

She leaned against a shadowy tree trunk in Central Park and waited for the inevitable. About halfway between midnight and dawn, an insomniac jogger bobbed past with her headphones turned way up. She was a cutie.

A lurker—not Elena—leapt up from where he'd been hiding just beyond the edge of the nearest lamplight. He tackled the jogger and together they tumbled a little way off the path. *Mm, Justice for dinner.* With that thought, Elena dashed into the fray. Before the lurker knew she was there, Elena had him in a tight headlock. He gasped profanity and tried to claw her arms, but she wore a leather jacket for a reason and it was only a matter of time before he lost consciousness. Elena waited those necessary few seconds after he went limp to be sure he wasn't faking it, and then dragged him off the jogger.

She took her first breath in hours to speak to the pretty girl on the ground. "I've got him. You should go find a cop." Usually when Elena said things like that, cute joggers got up and ran for their lives toward the nearest park exit. It gave her the alone time she needed to make her dinner "to go."

"I'd rather not involve the police." Pretty Girl climbed to her feet with a sigh and began rearranging her skimpy, now grass-stained jogging getup. She didn't seem at all fazed by the attack; if anything, she seemed annoyed at the rescue. "Can you just let him go? It's not his fault I was out here at this time of night, dressed like a cheerleader in heat."

Elena almost dropped her dinner in surprise. "Excuse me?"
She said it without inhaling first, so she had to repeat herself
before she got an answer.

"Look, just leave him, okay? He'll wake up in a few hours
with a valuable lesson learned. 'Don't jump stupid jogging
chicks in the park at night,' right?" She stepped forward and
made as if to take the mugger off Elena's hands.

Elena couldn't help herself. She snarled. Just a little.

The jogger hesitated. "Was that...a growl? Did you just bare
your teeth at me?"

"Listen, lady," Elena said, determinedly ignoring the
personal question, "you seem to be in shock. Or something. I've
got this guy. You're safe. Now why don't you run quick and find
a cop before he wakes up and bothers us again?"

"Because I'm not in the mood for pork, damnit! Why don't
you put him down so you can go get a cop?" Pretty Girl reached
again for her attacker.

Elena was taken so off guard that once again, she almost let
go of her dinner. "Wait, what? 'Not in the mood for pork'?"

The jogger got a grip on the mugger's collar and belt. "I'm
serious. I'll be fine. Just leave this guy to me."

"No way. He's mine." Elena tried to pull the man away
from Pretty Girl, but without success.

She pulled back. "I caught him, he's mine. Let go."

"He caught you, and I caught him. He's mine. You let go."

"I did not dress up like a fitness whore and go fucking jogging in the fucking park to leave with nothing." She was pretty
and strong, and in her anger, she almost wrested the mugger
out of Elena's arms.

But Elena was the bigger woman, and obviously had more
practice wrestling strangers in the dark. When she put her
weight into it, she hauled both the mugger and his victim a little
farther into the shadows. Then she shook the man to try and
dislodge the jogger. "Let go and get out of here before you get
hurt, crazy lady."

Pretty Girl was pissed. Instead of trying again to yank away
Elena's prize, she lunged at her rescuer and yelled, "I'm not
crazy; I'm hungry!"

Elena blinked and found herself pinned to the ground under the weight of an unconscious man and a homicidal woman.
It was a first for her, and her reaction time was slow. The jogger
was already trying to strangle her before Elena finally thought

to sit bolt upright, in spite of the weight bearing down on her, and croak, "Did you say, 'hungry'?"

It was the jogger's turn to be confused and squashed by the mugger's unconscious form as Elena inadvertently rolled him onto her. "What? Yes! Why won't you die?!"

"Because I'm not alive." Elena, didn't bother fighting the jogger off, she just rasped out the words in spite of being choked. "And neither are you, apparently." She couldn't help smirking a little. "Hi. I'm Elena."

After a second of shock, the jogger let go of her neck and scrambled off her lap. "Oh wow," she said. "Sorry. My name's Lucy."

They shook hands. It was awkward in all the usual ways and then some. Then together, they dragged the mugger away for a quiet dinner shared in an out-of-the-way place. It was magical.

Kay T. Holt is co-founder and editor of *Crossed Genres SF/F* magazine and runs the *Science in My Fiction* Blog. She also writes weekly for the *Geek Mom* blog. Her fiction has been published in *Tweet the Meat*, *M-Brane SF*, and the *Beauty Has Her Way* anthology from Dark Quest Books. She lives outside Boston with her giant husband, their genius child, and two monstrous cats. She loves science and art, and uses both in her writing.

SWALLOW IT ALL

JENNIFER BROZEK

"Don't worry, dear. I'll bring you back. I promise."

Those words repeated themselves in Susan's head so many times they shifted from language to babble to language again. It was something Paul had said to her. She didn't know why but she associated these words with pain. Not actual pain. Not right now. Right now she drowsed in that cozy twilight before waking. No, she associated the words with a memory of pain; pain that burned her throat and stomach. Why?

"I think we're ready."

It was Paul. She tried to shift, intending to turn to him, but nothing happened. Momentary panic flashed through her; body tensing and then relaxing. She was dreaming. Her body couldn't move.

"Susan, sit on the edge of the bed and open your eyes."

She had planned to feign sleep; tease him with a smile, silently inviting him into bed. Then she was sitting on the edge of the bed, looking at him.

"That's better. Good girl."

Panic rose again. She knew that look on his face—the one of smug satisfaction—and hated it. As memory flowed back into her confused brain, so did her hatred for the man she'd once loved. "What's happening to me?" she asked.

Paul's smug grin widened at the inarticulate moan that escaped her mouth. "That's so much better than all the shouting, isn't it? No more threats of divorce. No more disagreements. All is right with our marriage again." His tone changed as his eyes lingered on her mouth and he licked his own lips in anticipation. "In fact, it's time for you to do your wifely duty. Kneel before me."

Susan rose from the bed, took two steps to him and knelt. Her mind reeled in confusion at the abject need to obey. She knew she hated this man but couldn't muster the emotion to go with this knowledge. Instead, she knelt, waiting, vaguely aware that her knees didn't hurt. In fact, nothing hurt and that was a blessing.

Paul paused and looked to the doorway. "She can't harm me, can she?"

"Not unless you tell her to," the housekeeper and voodoo priestess said. "She's yours. She'll obey you until you die."

"Good. The envelope on my desk with your name on it. It's got the deed to your house and some walking-around money. I won't need your services anymore." Paul looked down at his patiently waiting wife. "Susan will take care of things from now on."

The housekeeper nodded, spared a pitying glance for Susan and left. She didn't need to stick around to know what was going to happen next. It always came down to sex in the end. The need for sex, revenge for sex denied, the honor of someone's sex stolen. No matter the reason for creating a zombie, sex was always at the core of it.

Paul didn't even hear the click as the housekeeper closed the door behind her. He was too focused on Susan. Good girl Susan. Never do anything kinky Susan. Always made a face at the idea of sucking cock Susan. Well, Susan had changed.

"Susan?"

She groaned softly at him.

"You're going to suck my cock now," he said as he undid his pants. "You're going to give me the best damn head you've ever given anyone. You're going to do it now."

Susan lunged at Paul's groin, startling him. For a brief moment he thought she was going to bite him but then her moving mouth and hands told him otherwise. She sucked his cock deep into her throat, swallowing around it, massaging it with motion. Her hands also massaged; one hand on his ass and the other caressing his balls. Then, dear God, she wrapped her tongue around his cock and licked. He hadn't known that was possible.

"Such a good girl, Susan," he crooned, petting her hair. "Normally, marriage is 'til death , but since we got rid of your pesky gag reflex, I'll make an exception."

She bobbed on his cock, ignoring the dripping saliva at the corners of her mouth. His hips bucked towards her as he started to feel his orgasm rise. "Oh, yes, Susan. Do it. Swallow it. Swallow it all!"

The tiny bit of the real Susan left inside the shell of her body heard his words, and though she knew what he meant, she focused on the words alone. She would obey. Oh, yes. She would swallow.

The first inkling that something was wrong was when Susan, her mouth still full of Paul's cock, bit down on his swollen flesh and tore the twitching member from his body. Paul started screaming as she gulped it down whole, no longer worrying about gagging or choking. All she had to worry about was swallowing. Blood streamed down her chin. She lunged at his groin again.

As she ripped his ball sac from his body and gulped each testicle down, she vaguely wondered at the concepts of "swallow" and "all" as Paul had commanded. Susan could not risk being wrong. So, as Paul crumpled to the ground, still screaming, she fell upon him, biting, ripping, and swallowing until the blackness took Paul. Susan, freed from her bonds, chose to finish out her husband's last command "swallow it all."

Jennifer Brozek is an award-winning author and editor, slush reader, and small press publisher. She has been writing role-playing games and professionally publishing fiction since 2004. With a number of edited anthologies, fiction books, RPG books, and short stories under her belt, Jennifer is often considered a Renaissance woman, but prefers to be known as a wordslinger and optimist.

TRAVELING A CORPSE OVER A THOUSAND *LI*

CALVIN D. JIM

I remember my first pangs of love for Han. We stood beside each other at his uncle's funeral procession, as the Taoist priest and his entourage left the walls of our town to begin their long journey.

I asked Han why they didn't bury his uncle nearby.

"For his soul to rest," he said, "his body must travel a thousand *li* to home."

I asked him why there was a red prayer talisman on his uncle's forehead.

He smiled and said, "To ensure he does not rise to become *Jiang Shi*, the living dead."

But his words didn't seem important now. Instead, I pulled his calloused hand inside the folds of my long *cheong pao*, hoping no one saw. I told myself I was only doing this to comfort him. Father would not approve.

# # #

Spring turned into summer; summer into autumn. Warm winds turned cold.

I slipped out through the servant's gate of my father's compound as the bell tower tolled. It was the Hour of the Rat. By now, the Taoist priests must've left their caravan to visit the House of Jade in town, no doubt to spend the strings of coins I had graciously donated in honor of the dead they carried. There'd be no one to catch me darting through the woods like an animal. But I had only a few hours until dawn. Less if Auntie Lin found me missing.

I crept down the lane watching for the tell-tale red lanterns of the night watch. Then, before I stole through the tunnels under the town wall, I peered back at the family compound that had been my home.

Compound. Another word for prison. Like so many daughters of *Qin*, I was political opportunity made flesh. More like a hostage whose ransom would be paid by a man I had never met, who would free me into a life of further bondage.

I checked the dagger under my cloak. I knew what to do. When they found me beside Han, swollen in death, everyone would know why. It was the only way to be with him forever.

I slid into the tunnels. Almost free.

# # #

I crossed the river and spied the crooked, old yew tree, barren of leaves.

Han and I had met there, that first time, in the heat of the summer festival, and our bodies embraced before we even whispered hello. We lay on a bed of soft grass, entwined under a blanket of darkness. Fireflies flickered like candles above an empty *cheong pao*, the rhythm of the water and cry of the heron the only sounds.

Afterward, we lay naked under the stars, his arms a warm mantle around my body. He called me his rose petal, and I asked about his life as a carpenter. He told me about his village, his mother's dumplings, and the many festivals they held every year to forget their lowly station. I told him that I wanted such a happy life and he said I was being silly, that I should not give up the place of privilege that was my destiny. I told him destiny held me in its snare, but had not yet trapped me.

# # #

The caravan was just beyond the glade; beyond the crooked yew tree. The rank odor of dead flesh seized me. As I approached, I gasped.

Han's body was tied upright on a bamboo scaffold, hung like a scarecrow. His once playful eyes had sunk into his skull, and his long hair swung across his face. Lines of torn and rent flesh, muscle, hung limply from his naked frame.

I gazed upon the horror of Han's misshapen corpse, realizing that he did not die the swift and painless death father had promised for the crime of violating his only daughter. A promise made to quell my fears and to prevent me from running away. A promise made only after Auntie Lin declared to the magistrate that my virginity was still intact, protecting our family honor. After it was clear I remained saleable goods.

But Auntie Lin knew the truth. And so did my father, thanks to her. Han had paid the price for that public lie.

The red and gold talisman affixed to Han's forehead was supposed to quiet his soul until he found his final resting place. But how could his soul ever find peace after what they'd done? After they'd ravaged his beautiful body? I took his pale hand into mine and felt clammy flesh. He no longer felt real. I wept.

I began to shake. Not in sadness. In rage. Through tears I saw my way to freedom, a way to be with Han forever.

I took the dagger from my cloak and unsheathed it. Voices echoed in the distance. Red lanterns glimmered just beyond the glade. Auntie Lin had discovered my escape.

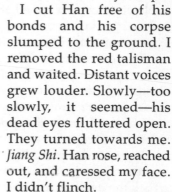

I cut Han free of his bonds and his corpse slumped to the ground. I removed the red talisman and waited. Distant voices grew louder. Slowly—too slowly, it seemed—his dead eyes fluttered open. They turned towards me. *Jiang Shi*. Han rose, reached out, and caressed my face. I didn't flinch.

"Rose petal." His decaying tongue slurred the words, but I heard herons cry.

Han leaned toward me, his body putrid. I dropped the dagger and wrapped my arms around him; felt his teeth penetrate the flesh of my neck. The pain was exhilarating. Soon I would be dead and soon after I, too, would rise as *Jiang Shi*. With Han by my side, we'd tear down prison walls. All the walls within a thousand *li*.

Calvin D. Jim was born in Montreal, Quebec, the only child of Chinese and Japanese parents. But he only speaks English. In other words, he is a truly Canadian mutt. Calvin writes Asian fantasy fiction and this is his first published story. While not sneaking away from home to write, you can find Calvin toiling away as a paralegal. He lives in Calgary with his wife and two boys, but no pets or garden gnomes.

DANNY BOY

RENÉE BENNETT

Do you remember? Us? The feel of my skin, as we tangled in sheets, as you moaned above me, a sound you'd taught me to love? Do you remember tasting me, love bites and nibbles, your tongue leaving a track of damp cool down my belly?

Do you remember the pounding fists on the doors, windows shattering? The clutching hands reaching, your shout of revulsion? The smell of graves scattering the aroma of us? I was screaming, screaming your name, dragging our sheets to the wall, as if a door might appear there, one without dead things behind it. I wept.

You yelled at me, "Throw me the bat from the closet, bitch!" and then you swung it like a sword. In your hands it was. It struck the dead down, breaking their fingers and arms so they couldn't climb in. Their faces lined the sill, teeth snapping, a round of enamel applause for your defiance.

I forgive you for calling me bitch.

"Leave," you said. "We have to get out." I wasn't sure why, with the dead stopped in the frame; wouldn't we be safer inside? But I followed you, lamb after leader, because I wanted to live and I wanted your touch and I wanted us.

We dressed and you dragged me outside, the air thick with their stench and their sound. They were dozens and hundreds, a city of dead raised in a night, hunting everyone, everything alive. You tried the car door. You'd forgotten your keys. You grabbed my hand and we ran for the hills.

The hills were too far.

Do you remember your harsh words in the dark, when I fell? You cursed as I lay on the ground. Said I was useless, a weight, was holding you back. I would be the death of you. You left me behind.

Did it hurt?

I tried to run after, alone in the dark, with moans all around me. I found a flat-topped gas station, doors cracked wide, the bodies all still. A ladder beside it, hidden in weeds. I climbed to the roof, pulled it up after, and lay on tarred gravel; lay there and wept because you'd left me for them.

In the morning, even the bodies were gone. They'd left me, too.

How long have I been here? Days, maybe weeks...living on gumdrops and stale potato chips and hope; hope that you'd save me, come back and collect me, say that you're sorry, and we could go home. Nights on the roof, the stars in my eyes, your face in my dreams. Calling me. Calling my name.

# # #

I awaken to your moan. How did you find me? Did you miss me, too?

I know what to do. I'd thought of it often. The oil-change pit in the floor, you follow me in. You're too slow to follow me out. The grating to cover it, I drop it in place, roll a barrel on top and fill it with sand.

You're staying this time. Staying with me.

Your eyes once so clear, bright amber in sunlight, are milky and clouded and gray. What do you see? When I move you follow, facing me always, but is it the sight of me, or the sound of my steps? My smell as I pass? I speak and you moan, like the love I once loved.

Sometimes...sometimes, I lie on the grating and whisper your name. Through the bars your blackening fingers flutter at my throat.

At least you still want me. At least there's that.

Renée Bennett lives and writes in Calgary, Alberta, Canada. She's had her work appear in such diverse places as CBC Radio, *Realms of Fantasy*, and *Year's Best Fantasy*, and she sincerely hopes this continues. This anthology represents a number of firsts for her, including her first e-sale and her first erotica piece, not to mention her first flash-fiction piece; the last fair boggles her mind, because she normally doesn't inhale in less than a thousand words.

SYD'S TURN

R. E. VANNEWKIRK

We take turns being dead.

Syd knows a guy, he sends us the stuff. She says he's an anthropologist or ethnobotanist or something, but a dealer's a dealer.

I order her facedown on the bed. She's perfect and cold right now. Dotted lines in dead ink tattooed by the pointed shell trace her backside; crawl up her spine like the stitching she closed my mouth with that time. But I won't do the same to her. I've had uses for her mouth this week.

This week.

I'm cheating. The deal is three days dead. It's been five and she's starting to smell.

She has small, almost shapeless breasts, a teardrop body, fabulous legs. Syd's ass is a heart-shaped, gray invitation crossed by the streetlights knifing through the shutters onto the bed. But right now I'm having trouble; I'm playing with myself and I can only get it halfway up.

I give up and tell her to make me a sandwich. She groans and I say peanut butter, bologna, whatever's in the fridge. She slides off the bed, almost falls on her face, and shambles to the kitchen.

Does this sound abusive? We take turns being dead. It was her idea.

We were watching that old Torneur movie on TCM and she leaned into my ear and said she knew a guy in Denmark who'd worked in Haiti and knew a real-live *bokor*, a Haitian sorcerer. I said it'd be convenient to know someone who knew how to make zombies, and we laughed, and I'm telling you it was Syd who said "sex slave" first, swear to God. She always was crazy.

I forgot about it until she came in one evening carrying a little box wrapped in brown paper and bound with string, about the size of one the boxes the bank sends new checks in. She sat on my lap and put her arms around my neck. The box didn't smell like weed but emitted a strong, earthy, fungal smell that should've made postal workers suspicious.

This is what *bokors* use to make zombies, she said.

Death is amazing. If it wasn't we wouldn't keep killing each other.

You lie on your back while she dances around the candles. Drums pound on the stereo. She chants, singing words in pidgin French we found in a book, sweating breasts lifting as she pirouettes. The pinch of stuff you drank with tequila and a lime fifteen minutes earlier kicks in, making your chest pound and clench, then she straddles your hips, dips the sharpened shell into a paste made from the stuff and dots your torso, your arms, needlepinpricks, breasts brushing your back as she bends to work on a shoulder.

And then the stuff kicks *out*.

The pain in your chest doesn't really stop, it...happens to somebody else who is you and you die.

There's a light and a tunnel, like on TV shows about people dying on operating room tables. A feeling of utter peace fills you as the last breath leaves your body and your heart stops, and the bliss never leaves, there's nothing to care about anymore. Not until the first pains of life return days later as the stuff fades. The first choking breath you take—you know then why newborn infants scream, and all you want is to die again.

Syd drops the plate next to me and it's peanut butter *and* bologna. Jesus.

I take her wrist. The skin is loose as a glove. I lead her to the bathroom and put her in the shower, turn on the hot water. She stands in the spray looking baffled.

I look away. I don't like how I feel looking at her face. Water like gelatin slides over gray skin and molds to her pelvis; the problem I was having goes away. I get in with her and am scalded. I have to turn up the cold. Then I'm pushing her against the sweating tiles, urging her stiff legs open, using my hand to get inside her. She's...*slippery*. I finish, then wash her. I scrub her thighs where my semen dribbles out. She *stinks*; not the musky smell like when she's been riding her bike, more like road-kill. I can't get it off her.

Then I tear her shoulder.

Skin rips and peels like cheap plastic wrap. Oh God. I try to gather the torn skin and just open a new tear. I've let her stay dead too long. I shouldn't have gone past the deadline even if she'd sewn my mouth shut. My mouth had bled for hours. *She sewed my fucking mouth shut.*

I wrap her in a towel. Wet skin like a popped blister is sloughing away everywhere. I can see where I tore skin fucking her, the insides of her thighs a redgray mess the color of expired meat. I make her sit on the bed. In the stray light from the bathroom, her gray parts are almost white and her red parts are nearly black.

I reach for the towel. She snaps at my wrist and sinks her teeth into me.

It hurts.

I jerk my arm away, taking a few teeth. I wrap the towel around my arm to stanch the blood and tell her to stay.

She doesn't.

She is off the bed and is coming for my face, growling low as she reaches for my head. I punch her. Sweet Syd. I love you, I'm sorry.

I thought she was clawing my face but she grabs the back of my head.

Her kiss has teeth.

R. E. VanNewkirk lives in Charlotte, N.C. with his cat, Elvis. "Syd's Turn" is his first submitted work. He maintains that *I Walked With A Zombie* isn't really as good as *Night of the Demons* or *Cat People.*

HEAD

WENDY N. WAGNER

I am not a ghoul. There was a time when I was not an executioner's assistant, a time when I wanted to be a doctor, a scientist, a man of reason. I sat classes at the Sorbonne for two years before my parents lost everything and I had to scrabble to find employment beneath my intelligence. But if I'd never been hired at the prison, I would have never been placed in charge of the bodies. And I would have never found her: my treasure, my darling. My faithless whore.

Sometimes I think just touching her was worth it all.

In part my demise is the fault of Jean Baptiste Vincent Laborde. I had heard him lecture many times, each measured discourse on the structures of the human body inflaming my stifled passion for medicine. There was something godlike about him, his brilliant and wondrous oratory. His words inspired me, encouraged me, and in the long run, derailed my life.

That fateful day, as I loaded the stolid, stinking corpses onto my wagon, I had no way of knowing how my life would change, how I would find myself imprisoned in the very establishment I'd served for ten years. I only knew, hemmed in by the blood-drunk masses, those peasant minds overwhelmed with post-execution excitement, that if they did not clear the road soon, the stench would become unbearable. Early September in Paris is still very warm.

In my frustration and without a thought for the ever-seeping gore, I snatched up the basket of heads and slapped it down on the seat. I climbed up beside the stinking thing and called out, "You lot—make way! Clear the road for the death wagon!"

I wanted to hurry. If I could get the bodies to Laborde within ten minutes, there was a chance he could use one of them for one of his remarkable anatomical experiments. But the cud-chewing rabble merely huddled more tightly around my cart, blocking the way more than ever. I laid about the wagon with my whip, but it still took a quarter of an hour to clear the square, let alone to turn onto the Rue de la Roquette. I was a good seven minutes from the doctor's house; by the time I made it, none of the corpses would be of value.

The wagon crept toward the cemetery, and I bowed my head low as my mule's. Inside the gates, I cursed the idiots who'd choked the city streets with their fervent, sweaty bodies. It was a shame that the Terror had claimed so many of our nation's best minds. We are a land impoverished of wit, grace, and beauty.

Without ceremony, I dumped the bodies into the stinking paupers' pit, but a fit of whimsy caused me to lift the lid from the basket of heads. What treasures had the masses kept from the good doctor Laborde? I lifted out one heavy cranium by its lank and greasy locks, and studied the furrowed features beneath the sullen brow. Not a promising fellow.

I went to chuck him back in the basket and saw a bed of golden curls he must have been nestled up against. I caught my fingers in the silken tendrils and tugged the blond head free from the rest.

I almost dropped her.

Such loveliness. Such magnificent beauty, even with blood smeared across one perfect cheek. The cornsilk ringlets, the azure eyes, the rosebud lips, upturned even in death. I could not snatch my eyes from her beautiful perfection.

And then she blinked.

Again I nearly dropped her, my hands stunned almost beyond my capacity to control them. She brought the tip of her tongue to her lips, as if her mouth were merely parched dry of words and not separated from the source of sound. I clutched her to me with the joy of a man who has found treasure in a dung heap.

The other heads I hastily discarded, but her I bundled in my jacket and hurried home. Water, yes, she must have it. And blood, too— that had been a highlight of Dr. Laborde's most recent lecture. Fresh oxygenated blood could keep her brain alive. The pool of blood at the bottom of the basket must have been fresh enough to provide for her on the journey. But not even a genius like Jean Baptiste Vincent Laborde could have predicted such remarkable function after that long trip to the cemetery.

I had to make haste if I wanted to preserve her. I darted into my house and set her beautiful head in a tart pan. Her lips looked blue. Fear gripped my heart and I pressed a quick kiss to her brow.

"I'll be right back—just hang on. I promise!"

The house next door thronged with cats, and the stinking beasts were forever having more kittens. The loss of one or two could easily go unnoticed. I caught two—a mother with a kitten latched on her teat. They were thin and friendly, but not even their eager purring could slow me. She must have blood, immediately.

I squeezed their juices into the pan without a second thought.

The blood more than filled the tart pan, but I caught the overflow in a mug. Her eyes widened, and the level of blood dropped amazingly—I immediately dumped my mugful into the pan. She was so thirsty. My heart clenched in my chest. I'd come so close to losing my precious creature.

I couldn't help but reach out to her, try to soothe what must have been terrible anxiety. "It's all right," I murmured, and brushed my fingers across her cheek. "I'll take care of you. No matter what."

My fingers, spattered with feline sanguinities, left streaks on the satin skin, but it didn't matter to her. She somehow pressed her cheek into my hand, her eyes closed in pleasure. I felt the moist velvet of her tongue stroke against my fingers. My breath stopped in my throat.

"Oh, you treasure," I breathed. I brought each digit to her lips, watching her lovingly polish away every last drop of gore. Heat shot through my body and I could feel my manhood straining against the thin cloth of my trousers.

Her eyelids fluttered open, and she stared at the bulge of my erection, so close to her vantage point. I felt my cheeks redden and my stiffness subside, but she ran her tongue over her lips as she stared at my crotch.

She stretched her wet pink mouth wide and made a tiny, demanding grunt. It was an invitation I could not resist. I fumbled at my laces and felt my penis throbbing in my grip.

There can be no words to describe the sensation of putting my most intimate organ inside that mouth. To look down and see those perfect lips wrapped tight about my penis, the cheekbones revealed by the taut flesh of her stretched cheeks, her eyelashes like bronze butterflies pausing in a field of white lilies...the hot darting motions of her tongue...the suction of her throat as I thrust deeper than any other woman had ever taken me inside.

Oh, God!

As my seed spurted out, the movement of her esophagus elicited a wave of pleasure so great I feared I might lose consciousness. She took every last drop. Her eyes gleamed with enjoyment. And when I finally pulled my still-hot member from her mouth, the joyous smile on her lips compelled me to kneel and kiss this angel of bliss.

I was still kissing her face, the decadent bow of her lower lip, the sweet curve of her jaw, when the hideous screech of my neighbor-woman broke my reverie of romance. The sight of her coarse face, those florid cheeks, those shaggy brows, her gums flapping as she bellowed unintelligibly in my face, snapped something within me. That such a thing should interrupt our tender moment! Such a harpy lay eyes on my treasure!

I launched myself at the ugly beast, my fingers closing around her wattled neck. The folds of flesh squooshed between my fingers in a most satisfying manner. Behind me, my little beauty clacked her tongue in a delighted, voiceless chuckle.

But even as the fat, old crone sagged in my grip, I felt hands clawing at me, blows around my head. My fingers were torn away from the flopping neck, and I watched my neighbor crumple onto the floor. I'd wished a thousand times to see her dead, but the reality of it stunned me.

I did not resist as they dragged me out the door—I could not look away from the corpse on the ground. I knew where they would take me—how could they not? I had killed a woman. I was a murderer. And there was only one ending for a murderer: the guillotine. Oh, I should have never touched those cats.

My treasure grunted and clacked for my attention. One of the louts snatched up the tart pan and all its precious contents, calling for the others.

"Put her down!"

They did not listen. Tears streaked my cheeks as I watched one man, dirty and mono-browed, lift my darling from her pool. I could not imagine what he intended, but I could not look away, either. I could hear the sound of the constable's whistle and each plop of blood as her neck stump dripped.

To my disgust, I saw her run her strawberry-red tongue over lips, tempting him, welcoming him. He clamped his nasty mouth to hers even as the constable pulled his wagon up beside my captors.

The ugly man held aloft my darling, calling his victory to his unwashed companions. His gloating was bad enough, but I felt my heart shatter as I met the smirking eyes of my beauty, my treasure. She winked at me and wagged her tongue in a dirty gesture.

And as the cart began to draw away, I saw him bring out his own fat cock.

The sound of her grunt and slurp still rings in my ears, even here in this prison cell. It is the sound of my own credulity, the sound of my demise. It is ever so much louder than the sounds of the prisoners on their way to the guillotine.

Grunt

Slurp.

Chop.

Wendy N. Wagner grew up right next door to a cemetery. It was the closest thing to a playground in her tiny hometown, which didn't even have its own grocery store. When she isn't writing horror and dark fantasy fiction, you can find her preparing her pantry for the impending zombie apocalypse or studying the history of evil.

RISK

FORBIDDEN FEAST AT THE ARMAGEDDON CAFÉ

JOHN NAKAMURA REMY

Adam hesitated before the shattered door, admiring the bloody handprints. Journeys into the forbidden were like this—crossing a series of thresholds, each one making it harder to return. When Takeshi looked back at him with those brown, bloodshot eyes and flashed that gap-toothed grin, Adam stepped over the shards of safety glass and into the fifties-style diner.

Takeshi certainly knew how to treat a boy. The restaurant captured the apocalypse nouveau aesthetic perfectly. Adam admired the axe and shotgun damage and savored the taste of damp smoke. His hips moved to the elongated screams and machine gun beat of judgment punk.

Opaque plastic canopies stenciled with "QUARANTINE" hung from the ceiling, engulfing each booth. Their waiter unzipped one and the aroma of fresh meat hit Adam and made his knees go weak. Takeshi's eyes never left his as they scooted their way around the vinyl bench. As the waiter zipped them in, Adam tried not to think of Sylvia and her uninspired casseroles.

Aperitif

They made nervous small talk until the waiter entered and placed two martini glasses on the table. Adam took one and inhaled a tantalizing human scent. The top layer looked like dishwashing bubbles, but when the froth tickled his lips, he could just taste the essence of brain. Next was a layer of blood, and under that, delicious, salty mucus. He drank deep.

It was like crunching into a face and experiencing the burst of sinus fluid, something he had not experienced since the rise of the Population Control Authority. As dangerous as the Apocalypse had been for Mortes, he had felt so alive. He watched Takeshi tongue the glass to reach every last drop.

His pulse quickened.

Salad

Adam thought again of Sylvia and eyed the canopy's zipper pull. He could just walk away. He had crossed lines, but not the line that counted. What if she caught them? Takeshi placed his hand on Adam's. They both flinched when the waiter brought the next course.

A papaya-half held a scoop of what looked like pomegranate seeds. While Takeshi spoke excitedly of molecular gastronomy, Adam placed one between his front teeth and teased it with the tip of his tongue before breaking the membrane. A tiny burst of iron-rich blood squirted out. The kernel was made of bone and marrow. Such cleverness! They ate the pseudo-seeds one at a time, allowing each to linger before letting human umami fill their mouths and spread warmth into their chests and bellies and groins. Takeshi held Adam's hand, firm but gentle. As his heart beat faster, it was hard to tell where the fear of discovery ended and the anticipation of the next course began.

Appetizer

The waiter next brought them a vulva. The cut went from the shaved pubis to the perineum and rested on a bed of romaine hearts. An erect, purple-veined phallus penetrated the crimson flesh. A pleasant musk scent, similar to the fear phero-mones exuded by Sapiens, filled the canopy. Adam was not sure how to approach this exotic dish. In privacy of their booth, they fumbled with their utensils until Takeshi pulled the penis out with his hand. The meat's freshness and the pleasure of dining together made up for their earlier embarrassment. Blushing and salivating, they picked at the labia and scrotum with their fingers. As he rolled a testicle around in his mouth, Adam realized then that he was committed. His choices had a momentum that carried him forward.

Main Course

Two Frankenstein-like waiters squeezed in, dragging a struggling and naked Sapien male. They secured the man with cuffs and cables so that he was bent over the massive table, chest down and arms spread-eagled. His neck was braced in the center. He turned first to Takeshi, then to

Adam, eyes wide and pupils dark, wrists bleeding against the manacles. The assistants exited and a chef stepped in and began to describe the specimen.

This human was in the prime of life. He was known among his kind as "Chuck" Bowman, and the cook personally selected him for his intelligence and excellent physique. He was the chief financial officer for a Sapien company that installed RFID tracking networks. He trained for triathlons, had attracted a voluptuous, fair-haired mate, and had three high-achieving offspring. Adam admired the shine of his salt-and-pepper hair as well his lean muscles as they struggled against his bonds.

Just several minutes ago, the chef said, in an apartment in the same building, Chuck had been engaged in coitus with his mistress, a nubile Sapien female employed by the restaurant. Not only was his brain freshly basted with the endorphins of sexual arousal, but it was also spiced with fear-induced cortisol and adrenaline. The technique had taken years to perfect, but the chef guaranteed the meal would be a singular experience.

The cook ripped the tape off the delicacy's mouth. The Sapien began to scream in rising pitch. Adam went rigid with excitement. He had to have this and he had to have it now and it was all he could do to avoid launching into an indecent frenzy. The cook brought a hammer down on Chuck's head in three precise strikes. The screaming stopped. He pried the skull open to reveal the soft pink-gray treasure beneath and then hastily backed out. Before the booth was even sealed, Adam lunged over the table's edge and was biting, tearing, slurping and gulping down pink flesh. Takeshi forced his way in and they were breathing, moaning, consuming. Together.

Adam felt alive.

Dessert

Satiated and drenched in blood, and with Chuck's pleasant aromas flooding the booth, Adam and his lover embraced. He felt the warmth of Takeshi's flushed skin. As Adam stroked his dining partner's black hair and wiped bits of brain from his square chin, he wondered what lines he would cross to feel this way again.

John Nakamura Remy lives in Southern California and is a graduate of the Clarion West 2010 workshop. Listen for "Forbidden Feast at the Armageddon Cafe" on a future episode of *Pseudopod*. His fiction also appears in *Broken Time Blues: Fantastic Tales in the Roaring '20s*. John blogs in various places and climbs fake rocks in his spare time.

LAST CIGARETTE
ARMAND ROSAMILIA

"It will fall off sooner or later." Daniel whispered because of his slit throat. He flopped his swollen member at Samantha. "I'm begging you."

"Beg all you want, but that dirty thing isn't going in my tomato."

They sat at the dinner table, Samantha smoking a cigarette while the holes in her chest and lower torso poured smoke. Daniel stretched in his favorite chair and ignored the fact that his left foot had fallen off at the ankle.

"Those will kill you," Daniel said.

"Even dead I have to hear your stupid jokes. This must be Hell."

"Why would you say that, love?"

Samantha laughed and pointed her cigarette stub at her husband. "For forty years I put up with you. Farting in bed, picking your nose. Growing into a fat blob."

"Let's not get nasty." Daniel glanced down again. "Just one more time, for old time's sake. Is that too much to ask?"

"It was too much to ask in life."

"But the rules have changed, love. You said so yourself the other night."

"I won't do it, do you hear? I'd rather die. 'I'd rather die,' get it?" Samantha pulled the last cigarette from the pack. "I don't even taste these anymore."

"What can I do to make this better?"

"Make what better? All you want to do is get that thing in me again. This has nothing to do with making anything better, just you getting what you want. I'm sick of it."

"But, love, don't you ever want it?"

"Of course." Samantha took a long drag of her cigarette. "Just not sure my last time needs to be with you."

"I'll make pretend you were joking." Daniel began to rise, remembered his missing foot, and sat back down. "You're like a sexual camel."

"Exactly. Alive I never wanted to do it with you, so imagine my mind-set now that I'm dead. I can probably count on one hand how many times we did it after Jimmy was born. Maybe you didn't notice."

"That might be an exaggeration." Daniel looked down at his rotting fingers.

"Jimmy was a good boy."

"Still is."

With effort, Samantha crushed the cigarette pack in her bloody hands. "I hope for his sake he's long dead. These past two weeks have been brutal. I hope my son at least died quickly and stayed dead."

"I hope he's alive," Daniel whispered. "Fighting the good fight."

Samantha smiled. "What's the chance you go down to the corner store and get me another pack of smokes?"

"What's the chance of you letting me in that tomato?"

"Get me smokes first."

"I don't trust you," Daniel said. "Besides, my foot's gone."

"Then I would get going. It's only four lousy houses away."

"Fine." Daniel pushed up to standing and began moving to the door, holding onto chairs, tables, counters, and anything else that would offer support.

The journey took almost an hour. The streets were deserted, fires rampant, and death everywhere. Luckily the convenience store was more or less intact, and he found a carton of cigarettes behind the scorched counter. Then he began the long hop back, imagining his reward. Death could rob you of many things but it seemed sex drive wasn't one of them.

"Here're your damn smokes. Meet me in the bedroom," Daniel said and tossed the box onto the counter.

Samantha beamed at her husband. She sat at the table and motioned for Daniel to sit. "We have a dinner guest, dear."

Daniel turned to see Jimmy, covered in gore and holding an assault rifle.

"Hello, father."

"Son, so good to see you!"

"Jimmy wiped the sweat from his forehead. "I was hoping to come back and rescue the two of you, but it seems I'm too late."

"Nonsense. We were just talking about you. I'm so glad you're alive!"

"I'm cleaning up this mess. We've already taken back most of the city."

"I don't understand," Daniel said.

"He's here to kill us, again, finally this time. Jimmy was always on the right side of things," Samantha said.

Daniel fell to the floor, as his other ankle collapsed. "It's not fair." He turned to his wife. "You promised!"

Samantha shrugged. "Jimmy, mind if I have a last cigarette?"

Armand Rosamilia is a native New Jersey boy currently living in sunny Florida, where he chases his loving children, bothers his fiancée Kim, and watches the Boston Red Sox devoutly. He has several releases, including an urban horror novella, *Death Metal*, from Sam's Dot Publishing, an extreme zombie novella, *Highway To Hell*, from Rymfire eBooks, and several short stories in places like *Twisted Dreams Magazine*, *Daily Bites of Flesh*, and more.

WAKING UP SOMEONE WHO ISN'T ME

MICHAEL PHILLIPS

I want zombies, the walking-dead, I want them to pound cold fists against my door, my windows.

I want to hear wood splinter and glass shatter, living corpses shambling and trampling toward me, to keep my company.

I want them to fall into my bed, onto me, cold fingers caressing, grabbing, pulling.

I want to feel the weight of living-death on my shoulders, on my chest, heavy and so right now.

I want to feel teeth and icy cracked lips on my wrists, my ankles, my neck, lovers who want me so very badly, whether I want them or not.

I want to feel teeth biting, tearing my flesh, skin, and muscle separating from bones, pain that means I'm alive, alive until it stops.

I want to feel warm blood running down my arms, my entire body, pooling around me, soaking ruffled sheets.

I want to close my eyes and wake up someone who isn't me.

Michael Phillips is an odd fellow from Tampa, Florida, who manages to write dark works of fiction that are strangely beautiful, and when zombies are involved, his work is disturbingly erotic. At least, that's what people tell him. His writing is deeply inspired by M, whom he loves beyond measure.

DATE NIGHT

PETE "PATCH" ALBERTI

There was black earth under her fingernails, and her knuckles were caked in dried blood. She closed her eyes and inhaled the smell of it. Wet soil, the iron tang of the blood, an overtone of decay.

She turned on the tap and rinsed her hands gently in the kitchen sink. Warm water, tinged black and red, splashed across the white porcelain, and swirled down the silver drain.

Her hands left rusty stains on her white and blue checkered dish towel when she dried them.

She could hear him approaching, with shuffling steps, and then he was behind her. He put his arms around her waist, his movements jerky and awkward. She turned in to him; inhaled him. He smelled like the smells on her hands, but stronger, mixed with something faint and musky and familiar. His old smell.

She looked up into his eyes, felt his lips, cracked and dry and dirty. He tried to speak, shape words with the tatters of his tongue. She put her fingers to his lips.

"Quiet, my love" she said. "Come to bed now."

She turned off the kitchen light. The magic still flowed through her and she could see clearly, her dilated pupils drinking in the moonlight streaming through the windows. She took his hand and guided him through shadows and pools of light, across the dining room, up the stairs. The step at the top squeaked softly as she passed; groaned at his heavy tread.

She'd left the bedroom window open. Chill night air, still damp with the rain from earlier, blew gently through the gauzy curtains. She put a record on the old player, turned the volume down. They danced to the low music.

He could still dance, in his own, slow way. She held him tight, as their feet shuffled on the deep carpet, and he held her in turn, rigid arms about her waist.

It was cold in the bedroom. He was cold. She embraced the cold as she kissed his yielding, slightly rubbery lips, then pulled away to unbutton her blouse.

He was eager now. He reached to help her. His hands were strong, but imprecise. The fabric tore, and fell away. She wiggled her skirt off of her hips.

He had been naked since she'd unearthed him. She reached between his legs.

It took more magic, an incantation muttered beneath her breath, to mold what was there into something useful. The power buzzed through them, sent tingles racing up and down her skin.

His eyes glowed with the light of it. He groaned, flung his head back, let sound without words escape his throat. He pushed her back on the bed, pinned her arms roughly above her head, and thrust himself inside of her.

She was not in control now, but that was expected; was what she wanted. She closed her eyes; let him move her as he wanted to move her.

He was clumsier than he had been once. He expressed his intentions in crude motions, broad gestures. But he knew her still, knew her body, knew what she wanted.

He let one of her hands free, and opened his mouth. She thrust her fingers deep inside the opening to wet them on what she found there, then pushed her hand down hard on her mons. Her slick fingers found her clitoris.

She gripped him as she orgasmed. He threw his head back and howled.

They fell back on the bed, slick with fluids. He held her in cold, strong arms.

She missed his heartbeat.

The magic began to fade. She could feel it draining away, little glimmers of light and life, skittering out the window, into the night.

"I'm sorry my love," she said, "You cannot stay."

She led him out of the house, across the garden, into the woods, the night air slipping across her bare skin, tickling her pubic hair, crinkling her nipples.

Here was the black hole in the earth. Beside it a pile of dirt and a shovel, ritual candles, mortar and pestle, and the dead girl, eviscerated, entrails glistening in the moonlight.

She lay him back in the hole, covered him with damp earth. The other body, she buried farther out in the woods.

The moon had gone down by the time she was done. It was cold, and dark; she made her way home as the last shimmers of magic drained out of her eyes.

She did not wash her hands. The scent of their bodies was still on her fingers, mingled with dirt and blood and toil. The bed was laced with the fading musk of their lovemaking. She closed her eyes as she lay down, and thought she could feel him pressed up against her.

It was getting more difficult. The ritual had taken longer this time; the ingredients harder to find. Townsfolk were growing wary of walking alone at night. But she would begin again. See him again.

Pete "Patch" Alberti shares a small apartment with two cats, one human, and the reanimated corpses of all his past lovers. The stench gets to him sometimes, but it's better—anything is better—than letting go.

MY SUMMER ROMANCE

SARAH GOSLEE

Kate and I used to walk along the shore, sand yielding underfoot and waves licking around our bare toes. Under starlight, no one could see us together, fingers entwined. That first night on the beach she turned toward me, reaching out, her eyes blank masks of reflected moonlight. Her fingers were tentative on my breast, as if expecting something other than soft, female flesh.

I met her through a personal ad on craigslist: "SWF, Z-curious, looking for a girl like me but different. No maggots please." I suggested we meet at the beach. Kate thought it was romantic. I wanted the fresh salt air to carry the warm spicy scent of her brains far away. I longed to taste her all over before I'd even so much as said hello. I hadn't been laid for months, and I was craving contact.

I could handle it, or so I told myself. That first night it was true. Kate touched me and didn't pull away, her hands strong and warm and experienced, her skin white against my cool belly, sliding down thighs that were now the green of the sky before a tornado hits. I expected her to be a thrill seeker, merely looking for another notch on her belt, but she emailed me the next day. We met behind the boardwalk after the sun went down. A pack of teenage boys saw me for what I was and spat on me, but I rinsed it off in the surf before Kate arrived.

The moon bobbed and weaved through the masts in the harbor. The grassy sward by the old lighthouse wall smelled of roses. Kate refused to kiss me, but her hands were eager. She laughed when I ran my tongue along the crease of her neck. I had to pull my head away, let the sea breeze wash her tantalizing scent from my nostrils.

Sometimes we walked afterward, along the beach and out on the jetty, an ocean of salt and seaweed and teeming invertebrate life. Kate told me about her job, her family, her plans. Her life had no room for me after summer was over. Her Halloween party might be a great hit if I were there, but how could you bring a zombie girlfriend home for Thanksgiving? Kate wanted to paint. I wanted to postpone the day I found my first maggot as long as possible.

Kate and I walked along the beach every night for weeks, ankles wreathed in frothing waves, until the night she finally dared kiss me. I smelled of hope, my mouthwash and breath mints covering up all but the slightest hint of decay. Just then I loved Kate more than anyone I'd known when I was alive. Her face pressed against mine, cheek to cheek like a bad romance movie.

The wind stopped. My teeth met in her cheek with a snap. The hot salty blood pouring into my mouth was the best thing I'd ever tasted: better than wine, better than sex. Kate never even tried to scream.

I feel strong now, toned, firm, like I'd spent the summer at the gym instead of hiding in a cellar. Strong enough to make it through the winter until it's time for a new summer romance.

Sarah Goslee is well on her way to mad-scientisthood, having taught her dog to purr and her cat to play fetch. She works in a mysterious government research lab by day, and writes speculative fiction and SF-related nonfiction by night. Her work has appeared in *Crossed Genres* and *Clarkesworld,* and she is a regular contributor to the *Science in My Fiction* series.

SECOND SUNDAY IN SEPTEMBER

STEVEN JAMES SCEARCE

In the luxuriant parlor of her family's palatial estate, young Bernice Lillywhite dropped her floral samples to the floor, her mouth agape in panic and disbelief. "My beloved Franklin was attacked? How did this happen? When?"

Mr. Lillywhite, her father, laid a comforting hand on her shoulder. "He was attacked outside the Hunt Club, my darling. It happened last evening. Mr. Michaelson, the Swiss man whose family owns the Machine Works upstate was the...ahem...biter."

Her mother, knitting quietly at the settee, raised an eyebrow and made a tsk-tsk sound. "He came—er—comes from a good family. Very wealthy."

"I suppose," Bernice replied, unhappily.

"You know that young Jonathan Stocksdale was bitten by their family gardener," her mother added.

Bernice scrunched up her nose.

"Terrible, yes," said her father. "Taken by a commoner."

Bernice looked up at her father. "Where is my dear Franklin now?"

"Just outside, my darling. His mother had him carted and wheeled to the house."

"I must see him. Let him in."

The double doors to the parlor swung wide and in walked the silent figure of Mrs. Havisham, mother of the groom. Their man Saunders wheeled a large animal cart into the center of the room. In the wooden-framed cart, lined with a bed of straw, was the animated corpse of her beloved Franklin Tobias Havisham, Zombie.

The Zombie Franklin gripped the gray iron bars in his yellowing hands and shifted his bloodshot eyes nervously about the room, coldly eyeing the occupants he now barely recognized.

Bernice put her hand to her mouth and gasped. "This will not do," she exclaimed. "That cart is entirely the wrong color. And it's used! Daddy, I want a cart cage from Sudbury and Gastogne."

Her father huffed. "Darling, the cost for such an item is..."

"I don't care!" Bernice interrupted. "I have decided upon silver and periwinkle as the color scheme and only Sudbury offers a cart in silver."

"Perhaps we could change the wedding colors to ochre and crimson?"

"Father!" Bernice objected.

"I am sorry, my darling. But that would better match his skin tone and eyes."

Bernice glared at her father.

"Even still, Bernice," interrupted her mother. "Whatever will we do about the wedding photographs?"

Bernice let out an exhausted huff. "Eaton and Childers is the best photography studio in the region. I was personally assured that any blemishes could be re-touched and made imperceptible in the final images. Surely they can perform the same kind of work to clean up Franklin's torn flesh, yellow skin, and red eyes. His cage."

Her father nodded.

The Zombie Franklin let out an aggravated howl and shook his bars.

Bernice rose from her seat and approached the cart. She remained at a safe distance. "There, there, dear Franklin. All will be well. You and I are to be married on the second Sunday in September and nothing will hinder our plans. Don't you worry."

The Zombie Franklin shot a gnarled hand through the bars toward his fiancée.

Bernice demurred with a half-smile.

The parlor doors burst open again and in strode George Alan Stafford III, heir to the Drury Flour and Dry Goods fortune, accompanied by the Reverend Gillworth, recently acquired from a small parish in Gilbourne.

George rushed to Bernice and took a knee. "Bernice, I just heard. I came as quickly as I could."

"Thank you, dear George," replied Bernice, offering him her hand.

"As Best Man, I am duty-bound to stand for my friend. If you will have me."

"That's sweet, dear George. But Franklin is well enough to stand on his own."

George stood and looked upon the remains of his friend. Revulsion crossed his face. He recovered quickly. Mrs. Havisham pretended not to notice.

George turned to the lady. "My sincerest apologies, Mrs. Havisham. I forget my manners."

Mrs. Havisham maintained her silence, nodding once.

George turned back to the Zombie Franklin. "Well, old man...it looks like the good Lord and your beautiful fiancée intend for you to be married after all." Leaning in to the cage, he whispered. "Bet you're glad you plucked the flower earlier, eh?"

The Zombie Franklin rattled his cage again and growled in a low tone.

"Spirited young man isn't he?" said the Reverend, now stepping forward.

"Yes," replied Bernice. "After years of planning, I'd say he's anxious to get our wedding under way."

Mr. Lillywhite crossed the room to the priest. "There should be no problems with this arrangement. Eh, Reverend?"

The Reverend looked at Mr. Lillywhite with a perplexed expression. Mr. Lillywhite held his gaze firmly and patted his breast pocket where his copious wallet always resided.

The Reverend nodded quickly and fumbled with his Bible, turning pages, seeking a passage. He cleared his throat. "Yes, well, the Good Lord, in all of his infinite wisdom and... mercy... may..."

Bernice interrupted quickly. "If the Good Lord found it wise to infect our beautiful countryside with the flesh-eating undead, I believe that he should have no quarrel with my marriage to the same."

"Oh, Bernice!" her mother gasped.

The Reverend, mouth half open, gave in immediately. "Yes, well... I should think not. I'll make the final arrangements today."

Mr. Lillywhite smiled.

"Please excuse me," said the Reverend, as he quickly made his exit.

"Well then," said George to Bernice. "I'll be seeing you both at the altar."

"Thank you, George."

"Would you mind if some of the Hunt Club boys and I take Franklin out for a bachelor's night? We promise to have him in his tuxedo and wheeled into the chapel on time, I assure you."

"No, please do. I'm sure he would love it."

The Zombie Franklin groaned.

"Yes, Franklin?" said Bernice.

Again, the Zombie Franklin made a frustrated reach through the bars.

"No, dear. Not until our wedding night," said Bernice, in a voice just loud enough to appease her parents.

The Zombie Franklin, irritated, shifted his red eyes back and forth from Bernice to George.

George caught Franklin's gaze and winked knowingly.

"That's it then," said Bernice, with an exhausted breath. "Everything goes according to plan. On the second Sunday in September, we shall be husband and wife."

The Zombie Franklin let his head fall against the bars of the cage.

Bernice was satisfied.

Steven James Scearce is a writer by profession. He is a former journalist and assistant editor for a Midwestern arts and entertainment magazine. At present, he concentrates most of his creative efforts on the sci-fi web fiction series, *Unknown Transmission*. He resides in Kansas City.

tAKE It OFF

ANDREW PENN ROMINE

Gina had made a good living as a stripper when she was alive, but the money was even better now that she was dead. She barely recalled the days before the virus baked her brain and necrotized her flesh, but she still loved the illicit thrill of the dance and the crisp snap of a client's twenty proffered from edge of the stage. There were plenty of clubs where she could dance, and at the rate the virus was spreading, more every day. The clientele was always a mixture of other necros and a few curious warmbloods who lusted for the mottled sheen of curvy, blue flesh. Their wallets were stuffed with cash.

Gina needed the money. Being dead didn't mean you could get by without the necessities: a roof over your head, brains to eat, an internet connection. So she dubbed herself "Bloody Ginny" and danced at Flesh, Rotten John's, and Bare Brains, five nights a week.

It was Friday, and she straddled a gore-slicked pole at Bare Brains, grinding to a DJ-Euro remix of "Sexual Healing." She glimpsed a big African-American warmblood through the fibrous haze of smoke, sitting alone at a table ten feet from the stage, draining what looked like five fingers of bourbon. His eyes were fixed on her quivering, pallid boobs. She didn't mind the stare; it went with the job. What bothered her was the houseplant on the table next to him. Who brings a fucking houseplant to a strip club? The leaves were long and skeletal, like fingers, gray in the murk of the club. The warmblood waved a Benjamin and Gina decided she'd pay him a visit when her routine was done.

A parting of lips that might've been a smile ghosted his face as she shambled over. She allowed him to tuck the worn bill into the microscopic band of her thong. Gina was too professional to savor the living heat that pulsed from his languid frame. Time for that later, she suspected.

"Hi, I'm Bloody Ginny," she purred, eyeing the tubular stems of the plant. They appeared more pod than leaf; bulging with internal orbs and terminating in a turgid head. She knew where this was going, and didn't mince words. "What's with the houseplant—you want me to fuck it?"

The client laughed, but the sound was pounded by the thrumming techno blast. "I'm Dr. Devin, nice to meet you, Ginny." He shouted to make himself heard. "Can we go some-place private?"

A doctor! They usually tipped well. She would humor him, both for the tip and to learn what the fuck he was doing with a potted plant in a necro strip club.

She took Dr. Devin to room five—it was a little bigger than the others. Some clubs just curtained off spaces and threw down greasy mattresses. But each private room at Bare Brains had four walls and a saloon-style door. An intimate haven, even if the ceiling watched with its hidden cameras.

Gina invited him to sit on the bed next to her and circled her nipple with a finger more bone than flesh. She felt only a dull scrape, but hoped she was turning him on.

"You want to take my temperature, doctor?" she teased, hoping he wouldn't ask for anything oral. Her jaw was feeling loose tonight.

Gingerly, Dr. Devin set the plant between them.

"I actually kind of do want you to fuck the plant." His laugh was sour with bourbon. He thrust one of the phallic pods in the general direction of her hips.

Gina shook her head. "You're even crazier than most warmbloods who come in here."

"Maybe. Is my money not good enough?" He thumbed a wad of cash—all hundreds. Easily $2K.

Gina tried to play it cool. It was a whole week's pay. She peeled off her thong but kept her lopsided smile.

"Okay, honey. But if you want me to do you, too, it'll be extra."

Dr. Devin waved his assent and pushed the plant closer. Gina thrust her hips and raked her fingers across her belly. Strips of flesh peeled back in loose, maggoty tatters. Damn! She'd have to be careful until she fed again. Devin gave her another silly grin as she carefully inserted one of the pods into her rotting vulva. The plant shuddered.

Gina didn't care for the bristly, invasive feel of the thing. She reached down to yank it out and the pod split, sloshing warm and wet inside her. She threw the spent pod on the bed.

"What the fuck is this?"

Dr. Devin stared at her crotch; his grin stretching into a full-blown smile.

"Take it off," he murmured, eyeing the dangling bits of skin she'd accidently raked away, "Take it all off."

Gina looked down to see the rotting flaps of her skin shrivel and blacken. Beneath glowed a flush of lurid pink. Morbid gristle sloughed away, revealing virginal expanses of silken skin growing before her shrunken eyes.

"It works! The silique of the modified *Raphanus sativus* are the perfect applicators!"

A tingling spread from the root of her spine to the base of her skull. She almost lost herself in electric pleasure, but something in her spongified brain recoiled at this reblossoming of her human meat.

"What kind of fucking doctor are you?"

"I'm a scientist—I work for the CDC. Ginny, I have cured you of the virus! You're going to be alive again!"

Gina didn't hesitate. She snatched up the houseplant and smashed the heavy pot on Dr. Devin's head, cracking his skull. Warm blood splashed against her newly budding breasts. Licking her still-pale lips, she pried open the wound with her sharp, bony fingers.

"Fuck that," she snarled between mouthfuls of tender, pink-gray flesh. She still liked the taste.

Andrew Penn Romine is a writer and visual effects artist living in Los Angeles, California with a wife and four cats (none of whom are undead). He is a graduate of the 2010 Clarion West Writers Workshop.

OBLIGATE CANNIBAL

KAY T. HOLT

Jared dangled limply from a sling while the lower half of his body chilled in a vat of solidifying gel. "Have you considered replacing this stuff with something opaque?"

Doctor Nava Levian smiled up at her patient. "Transparency lets us spot flaws in the mold as the gel sets up. If you're uncomfortable, we can draw a curtain around you."

"No, I like watching you work. I just hope looking at my figure all morning doesn't ruin your appetite, because I texted for pizza delivery."

The doctor and her assistant chuckled easily with him and went back to their other projects after eyeing his vat for trapped air and other artifacts.

They finished their pipetting even as the pizza arrived, and after sanitizing her hands twice, Nava climbed a stepladder to lock a tray onto the forward edge of Jared's vat. She chatted with him about the recent World Cup results until her assistant, Helen, returned victorious with a pizza cutter from the lab's little-used break room, and then the doctor excused herself.

"Mm, looks like the pizza chef topped this pie with the salad bar," said Helen as she sliced and served. "You're so athletic; I thought I'd have to pick off some pepperoni, at least."

Jared smirked back at her. "Nah, I'm vegetarian, too. My
students think it's funny until I lap them a couple times on the
track." He looked pointedly across the room at his wheelchair.
"After the accident, they must've figured I'd slow down some,
but so far that's only true on the soccer field."

"Ah! Now I know what Nava meant when she called your
new legs a '*fútbol* special.'"

Smiling, he hooked a thumb towards the door that Dr.
Levian had exited through. "I was hoping we could talk more
about the specs, but she's been gone a while. Doesn't she like
pizza?"

Helen shook her head. "I'm sure she would, but she's an
obligate cannibal. And she's too much of a lady to put that
much strain on mealtime conversation."

As if on cue, the doctor reentered the lab carrying what
resembled a cherry popsicle. "Out of respect for the dead, I
usually eat alone."

Jared swallowed thoughtfully and said, "Right."

"Don't worry—nobody was harmed in the creation of this
bloodsicle," said Nava.

Helen beamed. "I'm fairly proud of those, actually. It's my
blood and my invention."

"I'll be forever in her debt. I didn't know what I was missing before Helen came along." Nava asked, "Will it bother
you?"

"If you eat? No, I'm glad you came back." Jared took
another bite of pizza as if to emphasize his acceptance. Still
chewing, he said, "I knew what I was getting into when I signed
that informed consent."

"I'm glad."

After a pleasant pause which lasted the length of a
bloodsicle and a second slice of pizza, Helen punctured the
moment with cheer. "I think your mold has set! We can cut you
out of the gel after lunch and you can be on your way."

"Really? I thought it would take all day."

Nava smiled at his obvious disappointment. "I'm sorry. If
we'd known you would enjoy it, we wouldn't have mixed a
quick-drying batch."

She caught him blushing, but he paid her back in kind by
saying, "The gel's nice, but the company's better."

After they had cut Jared from the mold and sent him on his
way to a consultation with their favorite surgeon, Helen
elbowed Nava in the ribs. "He likes you."

The doctor elbowed as good as she got, but said nothing. "If you don't jump him, I will."

Nava growled.

"Don't get testy, get laid." Helen disposed of the remains of lunch in good-natured silence, but as she headed for the cold room, she said, "You know, it's not very often you meet a guy who'll sign away his legs to you one day, and flirt with you the next. Ask him out."

Nava chewed on the bloodsicle stick thoughtfully, but didn't promise anything.

# # #

The surgery was a success and Jared's recovery was speedy. During his next visit to the laboratory, he joked, "I lost thirty pounds overnight and now I feel like a million dollars...worth of medical bills."

That drew laughter from Helen who waved her nimble prosthetic hands in understanding. "Nava made my first pair almost ten years ago, and I'm still paying the medical center for the privilege of working here as a lab rat," she said with a wink.

"What, no employee discounts?"

"I get free upgrades. And like all of Nava's special projects, my hands are unique works of art." She let him admire their full articulation and the tiny loops and whorls on each soft fingertip.

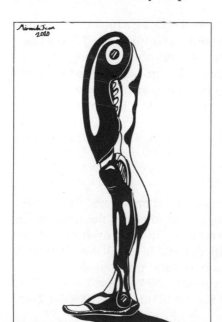

"The only thing I can't do with these is feel pain, and I don't consider that a loss."

Jared sat back in his wheelchair and sighed. "I don't know if I need legs as fine as your hands—if they get me back on the soccer field, I'll be happy. But Doctor Levian sure does do nice work."

"You can call me Nava, if you like."

Jared turned around to find the doctor in the doorway cradling a pair of high-tech limbs. They were shiny and gorgeous like Helen's hands, but where her prosthetics were white with pearl accents, his legs were black and chrome. "They look better than a new sports car!" he cried, running his hands along their length.

Nava turned them slightly to reveal a surprise. "I tried to reproduce your tattoo. Is it all right?"

A chrome dragon flashed in the light and Jared choked on tears, unable to answer.

"I'll take that as a yes."

# # #

Another month passed, and Jared came to the lab for his third adjustment in as many days. Nava scolded him, "What have you been doing, running in a demolition derby?"

"No, just coaching track, basketball, swim team, and soccer." Jared grinned. "You made my new legs too fantastic; I hate to take them off even at night."

She snorted, but her eyes twinkled. "If you'd treated your flesh legs like this, you would've wound up in my laboratory eventually, accident or no accident."

He leaned as close to her as he dared while she worked on the delicate insides of his left leg. "So you finally agree this was meant to be?"

Nava blushed, but didn't stop tinkering. "The next time you see Helen, you can tell her she's fired."

"She's just helping fate."

Nava said nothing, but finished tucking a biomimetic, nano-mesh muscle back into place before snapping the thigh's black outer panel back over the leg's secret inner-workings.

"All that hokey stuff aside..." He sighed. "You're the smartest person I've ever met, and I'd like to spend more time with you. We don't even have to go on a date. Just walk with me somewhere."

"If I walk with you, will you stop treating your legs like a pair of piñatas?"

"Yes!"

# # #

To avoid making a spectacle of themselves, the zombie doctor and the pseudo-cyborg walked along the river in the evening. But one walk led to another, and one evening became ten, and before long they drifted, hand in hand, away from the quiet bike paths and into the parks and promenades.

"Everyone is checking you out," Nava teased.

He sashayed a little. "Who can blame them? I have great legs."

"I hope you don't mind that I enjoy being invisible next to you."

Without thinking, he put his arm around her waist and pulled her tight against his hip. They swayed along together like that awhile before he said, "I like you next to me."

Nava stumbled to a halt, pulling Jared up short.

"What—?"

She closed her eyes and breathed deeply before answering. "Take me home."

"Sure. Are you okay?" He kept his arm around her, but turned her around bodily and led her back they way they'd come.

Nava didn't say another word until they were on her doorstep. "You smell...wonderful." Eyes half-lidded and still breathing strangely, she twined her fingers in his. "I want to invite you inside, but there are some things you should know first."

Jared squeezed her hands and stepped against her in the doorway. "Is this another informed consent process?"

She nodded once, sharply. "You'll have to restrain me. I'm dangerous when aroused."

His eyes widened, but he was undeterred. "What else?"

"Absolutely no kissing. My condition is highly contagious, and infected males become mindless, violent disease vectors. Do you understand?" She fumbled the key, so Jared took it from her shaking hands and unlocked the door.

"All right, no kissing. Anything else?"

She dragged him across the foyer and pressed the door closed with his body. "You can't hurt me."

"I wouldn't—"

"No. I mean it isn't possible." She said, almost panting. "But I'd like you to try."

After a tense moment, he delivered his consent with the back of his hand.

While in school, **Kay T. Holt** was described as "incorrigible," and she's been a living definition of that ever since. She loves deserts far more than she enjoys desserts, and if the opportunity arose, she'd trade a lifetime eating the latter for a lifetime dwelling in the former. She's known for being maniacally kind and ruthlessly irregular.

RAUNCH

URBANITES

PETE "PATCH" ALBERTI

"I can't find my penis," Mike said. "How am I supposed to go to a fucking orgy if I can't find my penis?"

"Check in the sink," Leslie said.

"What the fuck would my penis be doing in the sink?" Mike said. Then, "Oh, right."

He picked gingerly through the dirty dishes, and lifted a slightly soggy penis out of the sink.

"Fuck," he said, as he rinsed off some stray bits of last Monday's brains and broccoli.

"Hey," said Leslie, "I'm not the one who washes his penis in the sink."

She came out of the bathroom.

"Wow," Mike said.

Leslie had patched the gap in her cheek with a chunk of plaster. She was dressed in a tattered, gossamer dress, and had rouged her nipples. She blinked at him through long lashes.

Mike inspected her eyes closely. "Those fake lashes?" he asked.

"It's microfiber," Leslie said, blinking again.

"It looks awesome" Mike said. "Really sets off your eyes."

"Makeup technology nowadays," Leslie giggled. "Now," she said, slapping his bum, "get your penis back on and get dressed. We're going to be late."

They took a cab. Mike unbuttoned his jeans and fussed with his penis. It made soft little squeaking and squishing sounds as he adjusted it.

"It doesn't fit right," Mike said.

"It looks fine," Leslie said. "Stop worrying about it so much."

"Shit," she said, a moment later, and dug through her purse. "Oh, good," she sighed as she lifted a shiny black card out of the depths. "I didn't leave it at home."

Mike patted his pocket, made sure his card was there.

They arrived at the old warehouse. Loud music thrummed from inside. The bouncer, a big guy with mismatched arms, and eyes that didn't look like originals, inspected their cards carefully. He grunted.

"You're good," he said. "Admission for you is $40. The lady is free."

"Yeah, yeah," Mike said. He fished out some soggy twenties. The bouncer took them, and held open the sagging canvas flap that covered the entrance.

They pushed through the tattered black curtains beyond, and entered the club.

"Aw fuck," Mike said. "It's a sausage fest."

Leslie handed him some lube. "A hole's a hole, you always say," she said. "Have fun."

She grimaced slightly as she looked around. Lots of shuffling forms and hollow faces here tonight. Lots of decaying penises swinging between fatty thighs.

She wasn't bi, but gender balance was always a nice thing.

"I'm gonna get a drink," she said, "You want anything?"

"The usual," Mike said.

She got anti-freeze for him, blood and brains on the rocks for her. All of the couches were sticky.

"But hey," Leslie said, "We're dead."

Daisy and her latest came in later on. They made a little group that night, fucking, and pretty much ignoring the rest of the party.

"I don't really know why we need to go to a club to do this," Mike said, as he thrust his penis into the Latest's ass.

"Atmosphere," Leslie panted, as the guy's tongue swiped between her pussy and asshole.

Leslie came with a shudder and tossed back the remnants of her dull brown hair, settling back onto the sticky couch. She reached for a nearby ashtray, and grabbed a smoldering, second-hand cigarette. Mike sat down beside her, adjusting his penis, which was slick with cum and lube and other squick.

Leslie took a drag.

"It's all about the atmosphere," she said.

They decided to walk home. Most of the neon streetlamps had died years ago, but there was enough light to see by.

Mike patted his pocket where he'd put his penis, wrapped up in an old handkerchief. Leslie picked the plaster out of her jaw as they walked.

"Did you have a good time tonight, lover?" she asked.

"Yeah," he said, "it was okay."

"Let's head over to Survivortown for a snack," Leslie said. "I could use some fresh brains."

"Mmmm," said Mike. "Braaaains."

They laughed. Leslie put her arm around Mike's waist.

They say "write what you know," and **Pete "Patch" Alberti** writes from extensive experience frequenting the seedy sex clubs of The Valley, where he's known mainly as "Big Boy." Some call him a bisexual booty fiend. Others simply call him mind blowing. None of this, of course, is true. Patch is obsessive compulsive and terminally shy. He kissed someone once, gave the germs inherent in the act a moment's thought, and had to spend the next two days locked in an OCD cleansing ritual. Someday, his therapist says that he might have a relationship; for now, he prefers to spend his nights with a bottle of hand sanitizer, and a good movie.

MITCH'S GIRL

CARRIE CUINN

The pink neon frame around the wall clock blinked lazily, showing Mitch had only five minutes until the official start of his shift. Ron was sure to dock his pay if the Thrust-N-Thump wasn't ready for business the moment the first horny fuck walked through the door. Five minutes was barely enough time to sweep the floors and get the girls plugged in.

When the motion-sensor alarm pinged loudly, Mitch checked the security monitor. He saw his boss struggling with what looked like the lifeless body of a woman; the bottom half of one, anyway. He leaned in closer to the screen, staring at what could be nail polish or could be the heavy pixilation of the video feed. Mitch wondered whether all the toes were still present on her left foot, the one without a shoe.

"Hey, man, give me a hand with this one," Ron called from outside.

Mitch scrambled out the reinforced door. He slid his hands under those pretty little feet, lifting so Ron didn't have to drag her. Customers didn't want scuff marks.

Once inside, Ron dumped his half unceremoniously on the counter, leaving Mitch to hold her up while he closed the door. The pale, bare legs in Mitch's arms felt unusually warm, probably from being in Ron's trunk on the 70 mile drive from Herman Horst's processing farm. Herman handled the chopping side of the business for anyone who dealt in corpse parts. He bought bodies from his own suppliers (no one asked who they were), decided what he could use, and in this case, had sawn off anything left above the belly button. For an extra fee he capped her too, which Ron usually sprung for because he wasn't too handy with electrical work. If it weren't for Mitch, half the machines in the place would be held together with duct tape and spit. As it was, only about a third of them worked perfectly.

"Put her in Number 8," Ron told him. "She can be the new Molly. The old one's getting ripe."

"What should I do with the old Molly?" Mitch asked.

"Uh...put her in 11, she can be the new Zomberella. The old one's definitely too far gone, even for Kinky Eddie." He laughed as he added, "Her leg fell off at the knee last night, man. Eddie was in there, going wild, and all that jerkin' around finally knocked her leg right off." He shook his head but kept smiling.

Mitch picked up the new girl, letting her slide down his body a little until he was holding her by the top of her thighs. He could feel her warmth through his thin t-shirt.

"Um, can you..." he paused to get a better grip on the still-moving dead girl. "Can you sweep up? I won't have time now." He worried Ron might notice his growing erection. Luckily his boss grunted agreement and waved Mitch away.

As he got to work on the old Molly, Mitch could hear the first customers of the night coming in for their ten minutes of fun with their favorite girl. They were always called "girls"— as if Ron was in the business of selling time with perky, young cheerleaders. Old Molly was definitely past her prime, with greening skin and blooming bruises on her thighs which would never heal. Mitch got her plugged into the converted pinball machine in stall number 11, its guts removed to accommodate her hips and ass. He adjusted the blocks to keep her knees up. Her boot jumped out and nearly caught him in the ear but long experience had taught him to be on guard for that sort of thing. He got her into the ankle restraints just in time to dodge a kick from the other foot.

"You've still got some life in you," he said softly, patting her knee as he leaned to plug in the jack. "Quarters go in, current turns on, and it's time for a wild ride," he said to himself while he worked, repeating Ron's sales pitch to potential new customers. The electricity stimulated the girls' bodies in place of their missing brain, causing them to writhe ecstatically against the hard flesh of the man inside them. Like all the other unquiet dead, Ron's girls could move a little on their own, but not enough to satisfy his usual customers.

The old Zomberella barely twitched as Mitch carefully placed what was left of her in the incinerator. He was always careful with them, always respectful, even when he pushed the button that ended their second life.

Back in Number 8, the new Molly teased Mitch playfully while he worked. She wiggled her toes at him as he tried to find a pair of sexy, sandaled heels that would fit her, finally selecting a pair with gold leather straps that complimented her pale skin. Her ten perfect toes, with their dark red polish, drew him closer. Mitch breathed deep of her baby-powder scented lotion, surprising himself by leaning in until his lips brushed against her calf. She didn't twitch away or try to kick him like the others did. He stood slowly, rubbing his face along the inside of her legs as he rose toward the place where her thighs stopped and her body began. She squeezed her legs slightly in response, encouraging him upward. His heart thumped.

"Oh, Molly," he moaned softly, his hand shooting down to unzip his jeans.

"Mitch, are you done yet?" Ron yelled from the front room. "We got Judge Kirlen waiting on Number 8, boy!"

The thought of that fat old man, sweaty and anxious, waiting for this gorgeous girl, brought Mitch back. "There's a fucking ruined moment," he muttered to himself. Molly tried to curl her leg around him but he pushed her gently away and hurriedly connected her wires. He tied a diaphanous blue skirt around her waist, concealing the metal cap and adding to the illusion of femininity. Stealing another few seconds, Mitch dared to slide two fingers into her dark recesses. He gasped as she tightened around him, muscles clamping down of her own desire. The electrical current that faked enthusiasm wasn't switched on yet. This gentle caress was all her.

"Soon," he whispered. He might not be her first, but he would make love to her after closing time, like none of the other men could. Molly's right leg came up an inch, nudging Mitch in the side.

Making it clear that she wanted him, too.

Carrie Cuinn is a speculative fiction writer, art historian specializing in Early American books and prints, and amiable raconteur. In her spare time she reads, reviews books, takes pictures, cooks, and sometimes gets a new tattoo.

LIBERATION DEN

DAMON B

Kel's gasps of pleasure reached him through the closed door and Joel cringed, knowing his girlfriend's body was surging on the tide of an incredible climax. He used to send her world reeling. That was until everything had changed and she'd read that fucking article in Woman's Health, or some shite magazine like that, about coupling with the Returned.

The Returned.

He spat on the concrete. Damn PR cranks made them sound like students who'd gone for their gap year to Europe and come home to "Welcome Back" banners at the airport. The ones he'd seen looked more like someone who'd encountered the wrong end of a twelve gauge and never found their way to accident and emergency. Yet some guru reckoned that these people had died, communed with God, and been sent back as a gift. Farted out of God's backside, was more bloody like it.

She'd convinced him to go with her to Liberation Den, and he'd made it as far as the room's entrance. But, when he'd glimpsed the shackled, moaning form through the doorway, and caught a whiff of the antiseptic perfume overlaying rot, he'd backed out. Now Joel stood in a shadowy corridor watching others pass by, some bright-eyed in the afterglow of their own pleasure, others giddy with anticipation.

She cried out again.

He covered his ears.

# # #

Twice more Kel went on her own. After her third visit, they lay in bed, cocooned in each other's arms. Joel's face pressed close to her right shoulder, where a wide strip of Elastoplast covered her skin.

"So did you fall or something?" He knew it wasn't a fall.

"No." Kel paused. "He, uh, nipped me."

"It fucking bit you?" Joel's stomach went icy and he started to draw away.

She grasped his arms and snuggled closer.

"Don't get worked up. He wears a muzzle. You know, those metal cage things they strap over the faces of collies, so they don't savage sheep? It has a small opening, just enough for their front teeth to graze you."

"Are you going to turn into one of those things in the night?" Joel didn't know whether the rumors he'd heard about biting were true, but if they were.... He shuddered and pulled away to lie on the far side of the bed.

"Brother Goran says if we accept these little kisses from God we'll be blessed. I want you to be a part of this. If you don't, well...I just don't know."

Joel stayed silent. She had to be fucking kidding.

"C'mon honey. Come. Join me. It's an adventure." When he didn't respond, she rolled across the bed and tugged open the fly seam in his boxer shorts. "It'll be worth your while."

She tried going down on him but his body didn't stir to her kisses. She flopped her head on his stomach. "How about a threesome? They keep some real bombshells on ice, cover-girls and ballerinas."

He pushed her away and rolled to face the wall.

# # #

The next evening Joel put on Kel's favorite show; some inane wannabe-pop-star competition. He made popcorn, even rubbed her feet. But her eyes kept darting to the clock, and she toyed incessantly with the bandage on her shoulder.

Finally she said, "I'm going." The words rung with finality.

She got up and headed for the door. Joel stared for a second at the remote in his hand, then followed.

They didn't speak for the whole ride across town, not even when they parked and walked past the bouncers into the bowels of the old warehouse.

Outside the cellar door Kel said, "Are you joining me for a threesome? I had Claudia thawed out especially." She smiled hopefully, eyes lit with a strange sheen. When he couldn't find any words, she just shook her head and slammed the cellar door behind her.

This time Kel's panting was much more subdued, until she said, "Take off her muzzle," in an urgent and frustrated moan, like those times when she had her heat up and he'd gone limp inside her.

Joel froze. He heard her shriek, once, sharply, but this turned into "Oh my god, oh my god, OH MY GOD!" then a sickening crack, like someone's forehead smacking concrete.

He charged through the door and found Kel on her back struggling violently against two long, hooked poles held firmly by massive Tongan bouncers, the hooks pressing against her neck and torso, as though she were a rabid dog menacing a council estate. He skidded to his knees at her side, leaning forward to embrace her, all forgiven, but was hauled back by another bouncer as she surged up at him and tried to bite his hand, bloody drool spraying from her raging, contorted face.

Joel noticed that the head of the female Returned had been broken; so severely that her skull had caved in.

# # #

A week later he drove to the outskirts of town and slunk down the same dank corridors with their echoing, inhuman moans. He needed to see her, touch her, one more time. He hadn't had the release of a funeral to say goodbye because she still lived. Well, *existed* anyway.

Walking through the final doorway was daunting, but Joel's doubts evaporated when he saw how gorgeous she still looked; bitumen hair framing her face and cascading over one shoulder, hoop earrings twinkling in the gloom. She surged savagely at him, only held back by the chains shackling her wrists and ankles to the wall.

He hugged her.

There were differences for sure, a certain clamminess to her skin and the metal of her muzzle against the side of his head as she moaned. His body thrilled at the familiar feeling of her curves pressed against him; like she was still there.

Wire brushed his ear and neck, and cold metal settled on his collarbone. He felt a sharp pain as her teeth gouged his skin. At first he tried to draw away, but a moment later he was tugging at his belt.

He couldn't control his straining erection to have her.

# # #

Two days later he visited again.

Damon B is an Antipodean creature who roams the world and drives out the tedium of a daytime desk job with tales of zombies, tattoo cults, and life after The Apocalypse. He also features online at *Macabre Cadaver* with his piece "Inkorporated."

HONEY

V. R. ROADIFER

Maryann tromped into the restroom with a bad attitude and a foul taste in her mouth. She went to the bank of sinks, cupped her hand under a faucet, and slurped water, swishing and swirling before spitting into the basin. She shuddered as chunks of flesh spiraled down the drain.

"God damn zombies!" she said, not caring who overheard her. "I haven't had a good fuck since the zombie apocalypse. It's all putrid decay and sloughing flesh." She shuddered, rinsing her mouth again.

"Bad date, sweetie?" The woman at the next sink caught Maryann's gaze in the mirror.

Maryann rolled her eyes as she touched up her makeup. "More like a series of them. I'm never going down on a dick again; no matter what a guy says, he's never in good enough shape. Then he blames me because the damn thing falls off, as if it's my fault he's rotting. Why do men let themselves go so quickly? It's been six months since I turned, but do I let it show? No. I take care of myself, like a woman does. Like you do."

She turned a critical eye on the other woman. She'd been turned longer than Maryann, but had clearly made an effort to keep herself together. Her left eye had blown out and was opaque but her right was a clear whiskey brown. Her hair had thinned in clumps but what remained was a luxurious warm blonde. She probably used something more than pancake makeup to keep up the unending battle against sloughing skin, but Maryann couldn't fault her that. A woman had to do what a woman had to do, even if she was a zombie.

"Your skin looks amazing. What's your secret?" The woman's skin had a dewy quality that mimicked life better than anything Maryann had seen since the last human was turned a few months ago; it shimmered under the fluorescent lights.

"Now it wouldn't be a secret if I told you." She winked at Maryann, then nodded towards Maryann's disheveled blouse. "Looks like you could use this." She handed Maryann a tube of flesh colored mastic.

Maryann unbuttoned the remains of her blouse, revealing still perky breasts, only now her right nipple hung by a few threads of blackened flesh. "Fuckin' zombie! I can't believe he bit me!"

Maryann accepted the wax-based filler with gratitude. She wiped off the surface paint from around the injured area, revealing the grayish-green tone of her own decay.

"I'm Maryann, by the way." She smiled widely at the woman in the mirror.

The woman laughed huskily, as if she'd spent her life drinking hard and chain smoking, "Maryann, eh? I'd like to say I'm Ginger, but my friends call me Honey."

"Nice to meet you, Honey. Is that a nickname?"

"You could say that."

Honey laughed again and a warm electric charge ran over Maryann's skin. She felt as if something momentous was about to occur. She hadn't felt that way since the beginning of her unlife.

Honey nodded to Maryann's breast. "I can help you with that." There was a purr in Honey's voice that wasn't there a moment before.

"Oh, no, thanks. I used to be an exotic dancer; you know, before the change. This isn't so different from applying pasties." Maryann giggled nervously; she'd never been with a woman before but could see the advantages.

Honey said nothing, just watched as Maryann applied the mastic to her breast and tugged the nipple back into place. Maryann was conscious of the other woman's eye on her but she didn't mind. It'd been a long time since someone as fresh looking as Honey had admired her, and Maryann liked being admired.

Maryann leaned closer to the mirror than necessary to adjust her nipple and apply cover-up around it. She allowed her other breast to fall out of her blouse. Her pose also showed off her stocking clad legs to their best advantage and lifted her skirt high enough for the other woman to see the lacy garters underneath.

"What do you think?" Maryann asked Honey, as she cupped her breasts flirtatiously. "Are they even?"

Honey stepped behind Maryann. "Perfect," she murmured in Maryann's ear as her left hand covered the uninjured breast and the other slipped under the skirt until she found the top of a stocking.

"You know what your problem is, Maryann?"

Maryann could only shake her head.

"You're dating the wrong caliber of zombie." Honey's hand moved upward until it caressed the edges of Maryann's thong while the other lightly pinched Maryann's nipple.

Maryann thought for a moment she felt her heart beat as she whispered, "Who should I be dating?" already knowing the answer.

"A woman with as much pride as yourself." Honey's fingers traced along Maryann's cleft.

Maryann moaned and pushed against Honey's hand, demanding more.

Honey obliged, clever fingers burrowed inside Maryann, thrusting in and out until Maryann was prostrate across the counter.

Honey went down on her knees, rolled Maryann's panties down, and spread Maryann's legs further apart. Her cunning tongue replaced her fingers and within minutes Maryann climaxed with a satisfied scream. Honey didn't stop there. She licked every inch of Maryann's vagina clean, making Maryann squirm and squeal as aftershocks rocked her body.

When Honey was done, Maryann righted herself on wobbly legs. She reached a hand down to help her lover up. "That was the most incredible experience I've ever had, alive or dead. Do you want to..."

Her words trailed off as she got a good look at Honey. Most of her face had liquefied like wax, leaving behind a skull nearly devoid of flesh.

The zombie looked up at Maryann with a toothy grin and gave a half-lidded wink as the scent of warm honey permeated the air.

V. R. Roadifer is a Northwest writer of fantasy, science-fiction, and paranormal mysteries. She gets her writing inspiration both from dreams and her real-life experiences as a Wiccan mystic.

CLUBBING

MICHAEL ELLSWORTH

Dieter looked up from his amazingly poor beer and caught her eyes again across the dance floor. Just like with the Americans in Berlin, here he had the advantage: he was foreign, exotic, with a cool that only came from the unfamiliar. The Chicana had a bit of that herself, and a small coterie dancing around her, but Dieter had a good feeling that he was the one she'd be leaving with tonight.

There was a lot of exposed flesh on the dance floor, bumping and grinding to club music that wouldn't be out of place at home. Sweat steamed up into a haze under the strobe lights. Dieter stood by his stool, bracing himself against the pressing bodies. He was ready to leave if she would go with—or maybe they'd dance a bit first. He could definitely get down with that fine ass.

He'd hardly moved when the entire club's attention swung to the entrance, gazelles noticing a predator entering the field. Something about the guy there just washed over the crowd. He looked like hell, with a black eye, a rip in his pants, and a big gash bleeding through his shirt. But his hair was slick, his gaze imperious, and the way he walked made it seem like the beat was following him rather than the reverse.

The crowd leaned back then surged forward like a wave, swallowing him. He resurfaced near Dieter's Chicana. She bent into him and he grabbed her—roughly. But after a moment of shock, she seemed to be getting off on it.

That wasn't dancing—it looked more like they were fucking on the dance floor. Her entourage was drunk, piss drunk, and seemed to be losing what little inhibition they'd had, grabbing and groping both of them and each other, while still more people seemed to be getting in on the frenzied orgy. He saw her shirt tear, and someone grabbed her breast like they were going to rip it off.

That was too much—he couldn't imagine she really wanted such rough attention, though part of him worried that she actually might, that he would be in over his head with her. America was crazier than he'd imagined.

Dieter fought through the crowd, climbing over people to get to her. Hands grabbed at him, but he shook them off easily in his urgency. Someone pushed him just as he reached her and he fell, knocking the Chica and her erstwhile partner apart. Before Dieter could apologize, she straddled him.

Breathing in her scent gave him an instant erection. Her body was electric, sending jolts of pleasure all the way to his spine with every touch. It was wrong. So wrong. Gloriously wrong. They kissed, grasping at each other with no care for their surroundings. Someone fell on them, and he pushed them off, roughly, without missing a beat. Then he was in her, deep, and thrusting. The thump thump thump of the bass pushed them together, and the frenzied roar of the crowd cheered them on. Already he didn't know how many times he'd come. Sex had never been like this before.

She pushed herself up, fingers in his chest hair. He could feel welts rising from the scratch of her rhine-stoned nails. She kept the beat, slamming her crotch against his with the full force of her legs. He could feel her pulling another climax out of him when her face slammed into his, breaking his nose. He jerked to his feet and her torso flopped off his chest. Orgasm took him again as her nether regions, connected to her upper body only by entrails, slid down off of his cock.

It was only then he heard the shotgun blasts and automatic gunfire that had ripped her apart, saw the mist of blood now mingling with the haze of sweat. He screamed, surprised that it was more in rage than fear. He picked up someone's arm and started beating his way through the crowd to an exit, any exit that was away from the crazed fuckers shooting up the place. People clawed and tore at him as he ran; bit him even.

The exit was packed even denser still with people trying to get out—some of them, at least. A knot of people piled on top of a gunman in a commando outfit, and he shrieked wordlessly. Were they...eating him?

"Mother...*Wichser*!" he screamed, pushing through. He wondered how long it had been since he'd eaten, swallowing back bile. He emerged in an alley. Fires raged at both ends, and the crowd was trapped between them. The screams and gunshots were hardly audible out here, but he had to get out. He pulled a body out of the mass in the doorway, dragged it as close to the inferno as he could, and threw it down as a bridge to freedom.

The body squished and shifted under his boots, throwing his balance. He tumbled onto his hands and knees but kept going, pushing himself up and patting out small blazes where his clothes and flesh had caught. He stayed in the shadows near the walls as he exited the alley. *Ganz verrueckt...!*

Events shifted in his mind as the night played itself over and over. The dude. The chick. The glorious sex, and the flesh pressing all around.

His hotel was down near Market, but he'd lost all track of where he was going. There was a smell, though—sweet and musky, like an over-ripe cantaloupe. Like food. Saliva filled his mouth and dripped, spattering on the street. His stomach gurgled, and he moaned.

There was a beat, entwined with the smell. He followed.

Louder. Dancing, sweat, and fresh, pressed bodies. He pushed his way in—

All eyes turned to him. He could feel their musk respond to his, feel the crowd shift. He could taste them. He bit his finger in anticipation. Rubbery. He spat the nub onto the ground. As the crowd leaned towards him, he knew. He was ready to give in to his hunger.

Michael Ellsworth read J. R. R. Tolkien at age 8 while surviving pneumonia and social isolation in rural Kentucky, and this resulted in a love of linguistics and fiction, where even the world is up for grabs. He went to college by accident. After sufficient convolution, he escaped to California and became a linguist. Sometimes he writes by accident. It's all Tolkien's fault.

SUBLIMATION

DON PIZARRO

A fifty-dollar DVD on Brazilian Jiu-Jitsu for beginners taught Alecia everything she needed to know about controlling the average untrained live opponent. A naked, reanimated corpse with only hunger on its mind was easy. She smiled, deftly brushing aside its grasping limbs and slipping them into manacles, one by one. Alecia originally intended to chain the corpse before raising it, but chose foreplay over safety, instead.

Still sweaty despite the cellar's chill, she stripped off her T-shirt and changed into the Catholic school-girl outfit that hadn't been enough to tempt Jean-Michel away from his work for even five minutes. He was too busy building his practice as the bokor of their lily-white, gated community. And she was through letting things go to waste.

The corpse's skin was as dark as hers, despite its pallor; darker than Jean-Michel's. That, and its lean, well-muscled body, weren't its only appeal. The lust in its eyes captivated Alecia. A different kind of lust, perhaps, but it was enough.

She grabbed a ball gag from within the large plastic tub at the foot of the table, and dangled it on one finger from its looped strap. She dipped it into an open Tupperware container of cow's blood and let it hang a few inches above the corpse's lips. A few drops fell. The corpse jerked its head upward, straining to get more. Alecia wouldn't allow it. She recognized and savored the same pained and pleading moans she used to hear from Jean-Michel. Moans that turned into growls of frustration the more she would tease.

Finally, Alecia lowered the gag and let the hungry corpse take it into its mouth. As it suckled, she tightened the strap around its head. She imagined its mouth was working her aching nipples.

Whatever momentary satisfaction the corpse got from suck-ing the gag dry faded as Alecia straddled its body. Supporting herself with both arms, she lapped at the corpse's nipples. With its chained limbs unable to seize her, its sole unrestrained body part hardened.

For almost two hours, it mindlessly thrust that part—cooler than Jean-Michel's but warmer than something artificial—into whatever Alecia placed over it. The corpse could not satisfy its sublimated hunger, any more than it could sate its more con-ventional desires. Alecia's hunger was another matter. That was satisfied five or six times, by her rough count.

When she could take no more, she slid off the table and staggered on shivering legs back into a velvet couch in the corner of the room. It was one of a growing number of items she and Jean-Michel dumped into the basement to avoid dealing with them. He never liked that sofa but she did, and hoped that her miniskirt had somehow gotten between her and the uphol-stery.

Panting, she lifted her head and saw the attention of the still-moaning and very erect corpse turn to the bottom of the steps where Jean-Michel was standing. He didn't look at her or at the body on the table. Just at a small saucepan clenched in one hand as he idly stirred the contents with a wooden spoon held in the other.

"I found this," he said. "I heard...noises. I wanted to make sure you were all right."

Alecia sat up and crossed her legs underneath her, making sure her skirt covered everything. "I'm fine."

"I knew what this was as soon as I smelled it. I was actu-ally afraid for you." Finally, he glared at the corpse. "A good specimen. Intact. Healthy."

After a long pause, he confessed, "I don't blame you. Not at all."

"I should hope not," Alecia said.

"I'm just surprised."

"Surprised? By this?" She gestured to the corpse with her chin. "In this day and age? You always were a little old-fash-ioned."

"Not that," Jean-Michel said. He lifted the spoon from the saucepan and smelled it. "It's this. It's so...perfect. He was re-vived with little trouble?"

Alecia stretched on the couch, got up, and stood between Jean-Michel and the table. She pushed herself back onto it, sitting beside the struggling zombie, parting her legs slightly, letting them dangle from the table. "Yes, he was. With a little tweak here and there."

"It's even better than my last batch," Jean-Michel admitted, with a half-smile. "Always tweaking, you."

"I had a lot of time on my hands to get it right."

Jean-Michel sat down on the bottom step and laid the saucepan at his feet. "Turnabout being fair play, is that it? I was too busy, and so you would busy yourself?"

"That's all you see here? Turnabout?"

"No," Jean-Michel said. "I see a lesson learned."

"That's what you said last time. And the time before." Alecia placed a hand on the corpse's smooth and muscled chest.

"This will be the last time. I swear," he said with a pained and pleading look, unlike the ones Alecia had seen from underneath candle wax drops. "Unless you think you'd be happier with a husk like that?"

Alecia lifted the edge of her skirt. "I almost think I would." She reached her hand underneath and pulled out the Derringer strapped to her upper thigh in case of emergencies.

Shielding his face when Alecia cocked the tiny pistol, Jean-Michel didn't see her press the gun to the corpse's chin and fire. She blew the smoke from the barrel and offered her hand. "But probably not."

Don Pizarro has been subsisting on red-eyes and gallows humor since 1973. His work has appeared at *Fantasy Magazine*, *McSweeney's Internet Tendency*, *Everyday Weirdness*, *Reflection's Edge*, and other places. He lives and writes in upstate New York.

CLOUDY WITH
A CHANCE OF
ZOMBIE ORGASM
ANNETTE DUPREE

"Damn lesbians!"

There they were, protesting in front of the KNTH station, and weather girl Poppy Lynn had to drive right through the throng.

Herman is such a dickwad, she thought.

Herman. He just *had* to go into that tacky tirade about "banging" lesbians when he thought he was off the air. Only, Jennifer, the tech, was an actual lesbian and it probably took her all of two seconds to put him back on the air.

Then Jackie, the producer, only marginally smarter than Herman, fired Jennifer. How stupid could you get? Didn't they know what would happen? Now they had lesbians in front of the station. Angry lesbians. Since Poppy doubted there were that many real lesbians in their mountain Colorado town, the local carpet munchers had either trucked in a bunch of co-eds from the college town next door, or imported them from Denver.

Poppy brought her Explorer to a halt and everyone stared.

Poppy had actually made a pass at Jennifer, just last month. The young woman was a nice little package; on the hot lesbian scale, Poppy gave her a solid eight. She'd seen Jennifer's shaved kitty in the gym locker-room, attached to creamy legs, a non-existent butt, small, perky boobs, and pixie black hair. If Poppy was going to lick kitty for the first time, Jennifer's would certainly do.

Unfortunately, Jennifer was past the college girl phase and into the gotta-find-me-a-domestic-partner phase. Poppy was certain that Jennifer pegged her for exactly what she was: a desperately horny straight girl looking to get off.

Poppy inched the Explorer forward through the crowd. If the lesbians thought she'd be intimidated, they were wrong. She saw Jennifer and gave her a little wave.

Jennifer smiled and turned to a co-ed next to her. She said something, and everyone laughed. The crowd parted, but as Poppy drove through, the protesters lifted their shirts, flashing braless boobs.

"Damn lesbians," muttered Poppy again as laughter and catcalls followed her hot face.

# # #

After taking off her thigh-holster and hanging up her GLOCK 19, Poppy ate dinner, alone and naked. She contemplated having a wake for her dead vagina.

She was coming up on an actual year. An entire year without some lover pumping away at her cunt, and six months since her dildo broke. Worn out from too much use, the end had snapped off when she'd dropped it beside the king-sized bed only she enjoyed.

A broken dildo was the last straw. Perhaps if she stopped fucking herself with toys, she would find a man who didn't smell, wasn't married, wasn't an asshole, didn't come in five seconds, and who actually understood what a clit was and where to find it.

Poppy's problem was that she intimidated the locals. She was tall, blonde. She had boobs and was young; had a job on TV. And she was the Colorado PR rep for the NRA. She even appeared on NRA posters at all the gun stores, police stations, and ranges.

She should've known that as soon as the posters went up, her cunt would dry out.

# # #

Poppy had never woken up in a panic before, but her heart was beating fast and she was wide-awake.

What was *that noise?*

Bzzzzzt!

Her driveway alarm. The house she'd inherited from her grandfather was set back from the road a good ways, the ten-acre wooded lot longer than it was wide. A long way to the road through thick woods.

Bzzzzzt!

Probably a deer. It happened sometimes.

Bang bang bang bang bang bang!

Poppy's mind whirled.

Distant gunfire. *Rifle. Automatic. Must be police. M4.* She glanced at her clock. 3:12 AM.

Bzzzzzt!

Then the outside motion-sensitive lights turned on. All of them.

Shit shit shit shit. Poppy jumped from her bed. She didn't remember grabbing her nightstand pistol, but found it in her hand as she tossed back the curtains to look out her window.

Bzzzzzt!

When the electrician (married, damn-it) had asked her what type of lights she wanted around her house, she'd told him, "Any bad-guy should get a sunburn." Her driveway was now bathed in sharp, harsh, white light.

Men. Walking drunkenly. Shuffling up her driveway. At least a dozen. *What the fuck?*

Bzzzzzt!

Poppy ran to her gun cabinet. She pressed her thumb to the lock, it bleeped, and the door sprung open.

She grabbed her defensive house rifle, and her M4, and quickly put the one-point sling on, suddenly remembering she was naked.

Bzzzzzt!

Poppy took deep, measured breaths as she made tactical decisions.

Her M4 was loaded with 55-grain, jacketed, hollow-points, or what her brother called "vicious little fuckers," in a 30-round magazine. She ejected the magazine and grabbed the 100 round BETA C-Mag (the "bug-out mag"), and slammed it home, her hand stinging. She yanked on the charging handle and spun around.

Two steps and she grabbed the phone.

Bzzzzzt!

She pressed 9-1-1 and send.

Beep beep beep beep beep beep. A busy signal.

For fuck's sake!

Bzzzzzt!

Bzzzzzt!

She grabbed her cell phone from the nightstand; tried 911 again.

Nothing. Not even an "all circuits are busy."

Wham! Someone tried to kick open her front door.

Bzzzzzt!

Poppy left her bedroom and turned the corner. She raised the M4 to her shoulder and the red-dot sight, already on because the battery lasted for ten years in an "on" state, popped into view. She thumbed the switch on the forward grip and the Surefire X300 came on, bathing the door below her in absurdly bright light.

Wham!

Bzzzzzt!

Poppy found her voice.

"I don't know who you fuckers are, but if this is joke you're all going to die! Come through my door and I'll fucking shoot you!"

Wham! The door fell off its hinges revealing a fat guy in his underwear.

Poppy shot him in the chest. The force blew him backwards out of his slippers. The sound was impossibly loud, but strangely, her ears didn't hurt.

Bzzzzzt!

Another man stepped over the corpse; this one wore a robe. "Back the fuck off! Back the fuck off! Don't you fucking—"

Poppy shot him three times before his body hit the ground.

Bzzzzzt!

The first dead guy stood back up.

Poppy stared. Blood pumped from his chest, squirted actually, and Poppy shot him again.

"Aaaaaaauuuuuhhhh," the man said as he fell.

He stood back up.

"Auuuugh!" He started shuffling toward her.

Bzzzzzt!

That's not a man on drugs, he's a, he's a, he's...

Bzzzzzt!

He's a zombie, a mother-fucking zombie!

Bzzzzzt!

It's the fucking zombie apocalypse!

Bzzzzzt!

Get to the car get to the car get to the car...

WHAM!

Panic. That was her back door.

Breathe.

She dialed down the red dot from its bright 4-MOA dot to a dim 2-MOA dot.

The Fat Underwear Zombie was walking towards the stairs. She put the dot on his forehead.

Boom!

His head exploded.

He didn't get back up—but the one she'd shot three times did.

Bzzzzzt!

Boom!

# # #

As far as zombie apocalypses went, Poppy was in better shape than most. She stuffed another protein bar into her mouth and swallowed it with a swig of bottled water.

While not exactly mindless, the zombies were sure stupid. She'd been shooting them for over five hours, from her bedroom door. A zombie would turn the corner in the hallway, and she would shoot him in the head. She'd made a pile in front of the stairs, but decided to retreat to her room so she could check her window periodically. It was always the same view: more zombies.

It had been three hours since she'd heard gunshots from town.

She was on her eleventh 30-round magazine. She'd numbered them with a Sharpie long ago, 1 through 45. She'd killed exactly 352 zombies.

Don't fuck with the weather girl. She giggled.

There were so many headless corpses in the hallway, it took the zombies time to wiggle through, and as soon as the path became impassible, the zombies would stop to clear a few bodies.

In between attacks, she had just enough time to do quick things like put in electronic earplugs that amplified soft sounds and muffled loud ones, stick Band-Aids on her reloading fingers, and reload. She even put on a white slip to cover herself.

The tide would slow. Eventually. She had over 8,000 rounds of defensive ammo, and 20,000 rounds of military surplus ball she used for range practice. She would've had more (her father and brother always teased her about her shortage of ammo compared to their stockpile), but ammo prices had been stupid lately. She had a spare M4 and even a 20" rifle of the same caliber. Pistols. Shotguns. Even a sniper rifle in .300 Win Mag. She had guns and ammo aplenty.

Twenty-eight-thousand rounds. The town population was just over thirty-thousand, but she knew she was okay, because so far, the zombies had all been men.

Unless, of course, every zombie in the world was heading towards her house. Then she was screwed. She tried not to think about that. When the zombies stopped, she would get dressed, toss everything in the Explorer, and get the fuck out. She would GTFO all the way to the family hunting cabin in the mountains. There she would wait for her mom, dad, and big brother.

It was a good plan.

Bzzzzzt!

She hated the driveway buzzer. *Hated it*. Suddenly she realized it had been over five minutes since she'd last shot a zombie.

Through her amplified earplugs, she heard a car.

A car!

She ran to the window and looked out. It was a minivan, driven by a woman.

Yes! They must've heard the gunshots!

The minivan door opened and out stepped the passenger, another woman.

Naked.

And another one.

She was naked, too.

Then Jennifer stepped out.

Naked.

Shit.

More women piled out of the van as if it were some sort of nudie-girl, clown car, and Poppy's every instinct screamed at her to shoot.

The rational part of her brain stopped her trigger finger. What was going on? Were women zombies smarter? Were they not zombies at all?

She doubted it. She doubted it very much. Each woman had a look blanker than a drunk sorority girl in a physics exam.

A male zombie approached Jennifer and moaned. She smacked him alongside the head and he shuffled off. All of the male zombies were shuffling off.

Jennifer disappeared around the back of the minivan and reappeared holding a white flag.

Jennifer looked up at the window.

Poppy had no doubt she could kill them all—but what about the next group of women? And the next? She could not guard the front and back at the same time. Obviously, whatever had happened had left some of the women with thinking capabilities. What did they want? Were they on her side? Curiosity ate at her.

"Ba, ba?" Jennifer shouted and pointed at the front entry, cocking her head.

Poppy opened the window. "Fine. Come on up, but if you try to eat me, spit on me, or inject me with anything, I will cap your trash. And no men!"

# # #

"I said no men!"

There were ten women at the head of the stairs, including Jennifer, and five zombie males behind. The men were busy moving corpses out of the way, which was nice, but still.

"No zombie dudes! No penis! I know you can understand me. Send them out!" Poppy raised her carbine on sore arms and took aim.

"Mmmm," said Jennifer. Poppy could've sworn she rolled her eyes.

Jennifer shooed the men.

Soon it was just the women. Up close, Poppy recognized them from the protest at the station.

She backed into her bedroom and the women followed.

Shoot them and run, her mind said.

They were at the bedroom door.

Last chance.

Instead, she said, "Jenny, what are you doing here? What's going on? Where are your clothes?"

Jennifer giggled. Several of the blank-faced lesbians snickered. Jennifer smiled at Poppy and handed the flag to the naked woman next to her, who handed her something in return. A digital voice recorder.

Jennifer pressed a button.

Poppy heard her voice.

"Hey, Jennifer, want to come over for dinner Friday evening? I was thinking of some risotto and a veggie stir-fry."

Poppy couldn't believe it. She narrowed her eyes at Jennifer, who looked smug.

"Sure, who else is coming over?"

"Just you. If you could bring the wine—that would be nice."

There was a pause.

"Oh, Poppy, I appreciate the invite, but I only like to date dedicated girls, if you know what I mean."

"Oh," Poppy winced at how pathetic and disappointed she sounded, "well, if you change your mind, let me know!"

"I can't believe you recorded me! So you came here to get laid? It's the zombie apocalypse and you want to fuck?"

Jennifer nodded enthusiastically.

"And what the hell makes you think I'd go along with that?"

Jennifer gave Poppy a look like, "You asked," and then looked reflective.

Jennifer motioned her to the window. She pushed out the screen and Poppy looked out.

Zombies.

Not dozens, but hundreds. Maybe even a thousand.

Jennifer waved her hands as if to say, "It's better than the alternative." Or, maybe, "All this too, can be yours." Poppy wasn't sure. Jennifer put her fingers in her mouth and whistled sharply.

# # #

Poppy stifled a scream when the male zombie appeared at her bedroom door.

He was also nude, and Poppy recognized him as one of the local firefighters she saw Tuesdays at the espresso stand. He was tall and muscular but now he was drooling. His skin was pale. And he was very erect.

Only it wasn't a penis between his legs.

Poppy didn't know what it was. It was slimy and shaped like a penis, only smooth and bigger. It had a mouth not on the head, but on the side of the head, like a remoras. It pulsed up and down slightly.

It looked like a boneless, slug remoras.

Jennifer bent down and sniffed at the slug, then motioned for Poppy to do the same.

"Ew! No!"

Jennifer rubbed her own thighs. "Mmmmmm." She raised an eyebrow at Poppy.

Poppy sighed. "Fine. But if it squirts anything in my eye, I swear to God I'll go all Rambo on your asses."

Poppy quickly tipped her head down and forward, sniffing, meaning to jerk her head back.

Except...

Except it was the best thing she'd ever smelled. She inhaled deeper.

Spices. Cinnamon. Peaches. Cloves. Sweetness. It was an amazing smell. It was, it was, it was...

A drug. Poppy knew it was a drug because her nipples shot out beneath her slip, her knees got all rubbery, and she really, really, really wanted to fuck. The buzz in her crotch was almost unbearable, and before she could stop herself, she moaned.

Jennifer ran to the bed and Poppy ran after her, unslinging her carbine and throwing it against a wall. She pushed her slip straps off her shoulders and it fell to the floor at her feet.

Jennifer propped herself on her elbows and slowly spread her legs wide. "Ba, ba," she said in a low husky voice.

Poppy jumped on the bed. She had to fuck. She fucking had to fuck right fucking now. Fuck!

Poppy touched one of the legs in front of her. It was warm. Jennifer lifted her hairless mound off the bed and wiggled it. A thought intruded on Poppy's horniness—*is this how the virus or disease or whatever spreads?*

She shook the thought off. Whatever it was, it spread quickly, and pussy licking had to be way down there on effective disease vectors.

"Ba! Ba!" Jennifer said in a begging tone. Her eyes were saying please, please.

Poppy knelt between Jennifer's legs and hesitantly stroked the woman's thighs.

"Mmmmm," Jennifer whispered again, and arched her back. Apparently, Ba Ba Zombie Queen was ready to go, because her thighs were wet. Poppy rubbed them softly, wondering why they felt hot, and then she could...she could smell Jennifer.

Jennifer's sex smelled even better than the slug dick, but still of peaches and allspice. Her wetness felt like peach juice, thick and slimy. Poppy brought her fingers to her mouth and took a tentative taste.

Sweet. Spice. Suddenly Poppy felt like she was in Jennifer's head, almost as if she could not only feel her desire, but that she was living it. She rubbed Jennifer's thighs again, and startled. She felt rubbing on her own thighs!

Only, nobody was on the bed except her and Jennifer.

She rubbed again and felt the light, feathery touch. Behind her, several of the other women moaned.

Jennifer grabbed her hair and pulled her to her sex.

Poppy buried her face in Jennifer's cunt.

She licked at the lips. They were moist. Jennifer moaned. Poppy moaned. The women behind her moaned.

The more she licked, the more she tasted, the higher she felt. And she was licking the other women. Licking herself.

And. It. Was. The. Best. She licked faster.

"Baaaaaaaaaaa..."

Poppy licked her way up Jennifer's pussy, and came to her little button. It was hard, and Poppy flicked at it, feeling euphoric.

"Baaaaaaaa!"

Poppy forgot. Forgot about everything. About her weather girl job. The zombie slaughter. The firefighter. The other women in the room. All there was, was in front of her; a, small, delicious, juicy pussy. She attacked it with her tongue. She licked it. She worshipped it and she owned it.

"Ah! Ah!"

Poppy could feel the muscles under her hands tightening, and she held on tighter as Jennifer started bucking her hips.

"Ah! Ah! Ahhhhhhhhhhhhhh!" the woman writhed and moaned, and it was all Poppy could do to keep licking as Jennifer and the other women came. Poppy didn't stop. She couldn't, she couldn't. She was licking herself, and she was going to come too, she was going to...

She couldn't come. The impending orgasm faded and Poppy screamed in frustration.

"No! It's not fair! I haven't had a lover in a year! Jennifer, help me! I need more! More! Give me more, damn you!"

Jennifer put her fingers in her mouth and whistled again.

"Uuuuuhhh...," said a male voice behind her and a heavy weight pressed down on the bed.

Okay, maybe that wasn't the best idea.

Or was it?

She looked Jennifer in her eyes.

She really has pretty brown eyes.

Cold hands on her waist.

"Please," Poppy heard someone moan.

Then she realized it was her.

"Ba, baaaaaaa... " Jennifer whispered in return.

The cold hands lifted her rear up.

"Oh please," she begged. The burn was terrible. It was intolerable. It was torture. She was being tortured. Never had she felt such desire. Such raw, unfulfilled need.

Squish!

The zombie entered her as if he had entered a hundred women from behind. His hips were cold but the, the, the thing in her cunt was warm and wet.

And he just left it there.

It pulsed. It got bigger. Then smaller. Then bigger. Then...

He started moving.

In, and out. Bigger and smaller. In and out. Bigger and smaller. Slow thrust. Slow pulse. Slow thrust, slow pulse. Slow...

His hands and skin, everything except the slimy slug stuffed in her vagina, felt like cold, raw steak.

A beefcake. Literally.

With a slug penis.

And it was the most wonderful feeling, ever.

Pulse, pulse, in, out, pulse...

Then the zombie reached in front of her and started massaging her clit with a cold finger.

She was getting a reach around. From a fucking zombie!

The build-up began, making all her previous build-ups seem minor. Jennifer threw back her head and was panting along with the thrusts, and Poppy started rocking back and forth, too. A slap slap slap sound reached her ears, and it was music.

The zombie behind her gave a gurgling hiss as if the added motion felt good.

Poppy heard herself grunting. She felt detached and razor sharp at the same time. And the build-up kept coming, a monstrous ascent.

Poppy moaned. She panted. She looked around. The women were lying everywhere, rubbing themselves, each other, some were even kissing passionately. The air smelled like cinnamon and...

The zombie, with his other hand, smacked her ass. Hard.

"Ah!"

She was going to come. There was no stopping it now. It was glorious. It was the best fuck. The best. The best.

"Ah!"

"Auuuuggg!"

"Ba! Ba! Ba! Ba! Baaaaaaaaaaaa!"

Jennifer shook and shook, but then sat up. She pressed her lips to Poppy's mouth and kissed.

Her tongue felt hot and tasted sweet. It tasted sweet; sweeter than her cunt, it tasted like cherries and peaches and Poppy kissed her back, it was so sweet and—

Pulse, pulse, in, out, quicker, quicker, quicker—

Poppy thrust her hips back wildly.

Smack!

She was going to come.

She was

going

to...

...

...

Poppy couldn't think. She couldn't scream. All she could do was give throaty grunts that seemed to come from her core as the orgasm consumed her. It rolled from her breasts to her clit and then deep, deep, into her vagina, contracting around the thing it felt so good it felt so good it felt so good...

She collapsed onto Jennifer.

The zombie fell off the bed with a gurgle.

"Mmmmmm... " said Jennifer as she stroked Poppy's hair.

Poppy turned towards the convulsing zombie on the floor. He was making pathetic mewling noises.

Poppy stared between his legs. His penis was gone. There just was a gaping hole, gushing puss, and a grotesque, mucousy substance from the ghastly wound where his balls and dick used to be. The zombie thrashed and was still.

Pulse, pulse, pulse.

Poppy's brain refused to function.

Jennifer flipped her over. She stroked Poppy's hair and crooned to her, softly.

The dick-thing was moving. It was pulsing up her vagina. It felt warm and wet.

Four other, zombie men entered the room. Four naked lesbian co-eds went to them, grabbed their erect slug-dicks, and yanked, hard. The things came off with a sucking splorch and the zombies fell to the ground. Puss and green ooze squirted from the holes in their crotches. They writhed on the floor and then were still.

She felt it ooze past her cervix. She moaned again. Jennifer moaned. The other women moaned.

It was in her. All the way. And it never
stopped
pulsing.

Poppy watched as feminine hands put a slug-thing on her chest, near her left breast. It felt warm, almost hot.

Another placed one on Poppy's other breast.

Her belly.

Her left thigh.

She was sitting up, leaning against Jennifer now with her legs spread, and the woman continued to stroke her hair. Poppy watched and felt the things move on her body, leaving slimy trails that glistened in the morning light spilling through her bedroom window. Where the breeze touched the trails, it felt cool, a contrast to the warm pulsing.

One slug latched onto her right breast and started sucking, softly. It was slimy, like lube.

The slug on her belly left a trail as it pulsed to her sex. It oozed down to her clit and oh so softly started to suck, sending little pulses of pleasure through her cunt.

Suck, suck, suck, pulse.

Suck, suck, suck, pulse.

The creature on her thigh pulsed to her outer lips, then the inner ones, and wiggled lovingly into her folds.

It wiggled around as if it was enjoying itself, as if her sex gave it pleasure, as if it was happy. Poppy, panting, noticed it was wet, wet from her juices, wet because she made it wet, wet for her.

It slipped in and started moving up, filling her, pulsing and pulsing, filling her up, making her more wet and...

Suck, suck, suck, pulse, pulse.

One of the things was moving back down.

Suck, suck, suck, pulse, pulse.

"Ba-Ba," said Jennifer, lovingly, as she patted Poppy's tummy with a tender gesture.

It slipped out, glistening wet. One of the women picked it up tenderly and held it out for the others to see.

"Oooooooh," several of them said.

"Thanks for changing your mind," Poppy tried to say aloud.

"Ponies," was all that came out.

Jennifer looked at her. "Ba. Ba."

"Ponies. PO-NIES!"

"BA BA!"

"PONIES!"

Jennifer slapped her alongside the head.

Poppy snuggled into the woman's breasts, smiling.

The woman with slug left, clutching it to her breasts, and the other women followed. Poppy could hear them go down the stairs and out the door. Soon the van started and she heard it drive away.

"Ponies," she whispered. "Ponies."

Jennifer giggled as Poppy fell asleep to the beautiful sucking and pulsing.

Annette Dupree lives on the Washington coast dreaming of the day she can quit her day job and have nubile cuties tend to her every need. For fun, she likes having sex while watching horror movies. *Alien* is her personal favorite.

THE EDITORS

Jaym Gates started out a writer, added reporting, administrating, and promotional work, and then made a joke on twitter and became an editor. Now she edits *Little Death of Crossed Genres* and is the Publicity Manager for Raw Dog Screaming Press, among other things. Unable to choose a genre, she labels her writing New Weird, throws it in the spec-lit bowl, and tosses it with dusty butcher knives.

Erika Holt had the good sense to abandon her lucrative career as a civil litigation lawyer to become an under (or un-) paid editor and writer of speculative fiction. She spends most of her time living in strange lands, accompanied by witches, monsters, heroes, and other creatures, but maintains a few earthly obsessions, including NHL hockey, music, reality TV talent competitions, and painting her toenails strange colors.

tHE ARtIStS

Galen Dara likes sitting in the dark with her sketchbook, mining the nooks and crannies. She loves skeptics, mystics, storytellers, and image-makers.

Miranda Jean is a varied artist currently living in Scotland. After long interest in illustration she finally came across the perfect opportunity to get involved...in the form of a zombie romance/erotica anthology. Miranda sometimes wonders what her brain is playing at and writing in the third person is not helping. She thinks she might go and lie down for a bit now.

Robert "Nix" Nixon left the warm bosom of his family in pastoral Ohio to take up residence in a decrepit, rusting Detroit warehouse. The volatile stew of his brain which festered with Russ Meyer movies, zombies, and hot-rods, has been tamed by years of design experience. Today he produces bizarre, creepy, and sometimes hilarious images that are distinctly his. He also likes bacon a little too much (if you catch our vernacular).